# Praise for
## Virginia Hamilton's

### *Willie Bea and the Time the Martians Landed*

"The author of numerous prize winners recreates a Halloween like no other in America — Oct. 30, 1938 — in the story of the 12-year-old Willie Bea and her closeknit kin....The day is full of funny and fraught incidents....The effects on Willie Bea provide ideas for thought, an angle that Hamilton subtly injects into a delightfully entertaining novel." — *Publishers Weekly*

"From heart-catching scenes of physical and verbal affection to candor about the complications of love....All the characters are strongly individualized, complex, surprising." — *School Library Journal*

"The story...presents both the adult characters and the tightly knit family life from the point of view of Willie Bea. What she observes and thinks develops into a pattern which at times touches on the terrors of the unknown but ultimately creates a quietly humorous and loving pastoral narrative." — *The Horn Book*

# Also by
# VIRGINIA HAMILTON

*Cousins*

*The Mystery of Drear House*

# Willie Bea
## and the Time
## the Martians Landed

APPLE SIGNATURE

# VIRGINIA HAMILTON

## Willie Bea and the Time the Martians Landed

AN
**APPLE**
PAPERBACK

SCHOLASTIC INC.
New York Toronto London Auckland Sydney

ISBN 0-590-12029-8

12 11 10 9 8 7 6 5 4 3 2 1          7 8 9/9 0 1 2/0

Printed in the U.S.A.          40

First Scholastic printing, October 1997

FOR ARNOLD

# Willie Bea
## and the Time
## the Martians Landed

1 "Willie Bea? Willie Bea?" Toughy called. "Guess what arrive in a looong, black 'n' fine motor car. Willie Bea Mills, you hidin'? You *hear* me? You people done come!"

Once tonight is night, Willie Bea thought, I'm gonna *lose* Toughy Clay. Why me? Why must I bother with the whole rag-tag end of town whenever somebody comes to visit? Nosey-body! Toughy Clay! And it's almost Halloween!

Willie Bea's anger rose.

"Willie Bea, Willie Bea . . ." The sound of Toughy Clay calling her went off in the distance. It veered and came close again.

Hiding under the back porch, she made herself as small

as she could. The time was a slightly cool Sunday on the tail end of October. A sticky, airless late morning everywhere except under Willie Bea's old wooden porch. There, the ground was weedy and shadowy. There were places where fresh moss grew. Willie Bea stretched out on her stomach so she could smell the sweet earth down beneath yellowish grasses.

"Oh, it's so nice!" Her lips barely made a sound, touching the moss.

I've got plenty of time, she thought. Begging for treats won't start good till it's nighttime. Plenty of time to get myself painted and the kids, too.

She never had to think about dressing up for begging. What to wear always came to her as she went about finding old garments for her and Bay Sister and Bay Brother to wear.

Tonight would be an exciting time of treats or tricks all over town.

Willie Bea stared at the ground. Suddenly, she was alert. Listening, she heard Toughy Clay trot into her yard again and run inside her house.

Like he lives here! Like he's my own family!

He came out the back door, slamming the screen behind him. He flopped down on the porch with his back resting against the screen. His rump and his legs were directly above Willie Bea.

She held her breath.

"Ummm," Toughy Clay grunted, breathing hard. When he had caught his breath, he sang out of tune, *"Should I may, oh, should I may?"*

2

Willie Bea held in an urge to giggle. What's he mean, should I may?

"Willie Bea! You people done come and they here over there at Gramp Wing's right now!"

Hasn't got the sense he was born with, she thought, closing her eyes tight.

Toughy Clay's mother was Honey Clay, the only hairdresser in town. She gave Willie Bea a hair-do for free any time Willie Bea needed one. As long as Willie Bea would look after her Toughy awhile while she worked. That was why Willie Bea's hair was always straightened and then curled to perfection every Sunday.

"There's Hewitt Wing come to town," Toughy yelled, on the porch above Willie Bea. "And he stayin' over. Say he gone beggin' with Big Wing, and you can't go neither, Willie Bea. And Uncle Donald, Hewitt's papa, is there."

Don't you think I know that? They're *my* relatives! Willie Bea thought.

"And Aunt Mattie Belle, Hewitt's mama, and they gone stay all night at you Grand and Gramp's 'cross the road. And Uncle Jimmy Wing's kids done already sprang over there from across the field. They all lookin' for you, too.

"And Hewitt and Big already slip off with you baby brother right under you mama's nose," Toughy went on. "Hewitt's papa, you Uncle Donald, already have him a highball twice—I know where you hidin'!"

Toughy leaped off the porch on his skinny legs. Willie Bea saw him stand still at the edge of the porch. He had on corduroy knee pants, knickers. And nothing on his legs below the knees, and no shoes.

Then Toughy was moving straight for the barn. The barn was the only outbuilding Willie Bea's papa had on their small farm. The front part of it was a shed. Jason Mills, her papa, kept his rakes and hoes there. The high stilts Willie Bea had made for herself and her sister leaned against the wall.

"Willie Bea, I know you here!" Toughy Clay called. He had opened the door in the rear of the shed, which led to the hog gallery. The hogs could come into the rear shed from the fenced-in field. They would be fed slops in the gallery by her papa. He would stand on a platform that ran the width of the barn.

Willie Bea wasn't anywhere that Toughy could see. He came back up onto the porch and opened the screen door partway. He listened.

Oh, don't you go in my house, don't you dare go upstairs and wake my mama! Willie Bea thought.

She'd forgotten Toughy had said her mama was over at the old homestead, where Wing relatives from Ashtabula would be staying overnight.

Why must they come on Sunday when I am busy with Halloween begging? she thought.

She knew why. Uncle Donald worked Saturdays. And this being 1938 and not better yet, her papa said, men worked when they could.

Toughy Clay let the screen slam. He jumped off the porch. He was going. Willie Bea listened to the sound of his feet dragging through the grass. She could tell he was headed over to her cousin Big Wing's house through the large field that separated her Grand and Gramp Wing's old homestead from Uncle Jimmy Wing's farm.

Uncle Jimmy Wing was her mama's brother. His wife was Lucille Long Wing. Uncle Jimmy and Aunt Lucille's children were Big and Little Wing. Those were their real names—Big and Little.

Willie Bea's family farm was directly across the road from Grand and Gramp Wing's homestead. Their family house was on a line with Uncle Jimmy and Aunt Lucille Wing's house, on opposite sides of the five-acre field owned by Jimmy and Lucille. Aunt Lucille was most often called Aunt Lu. Uncle Jimmy was that to everyone. He was the best farmer in the family. He had two barns on his property; one of them was huge. He would allow no electricity in his house. He'd heard it was the devil's power.

Jason Mills, Willie Bea's papa, was the worst farmer in the family. But to Willie Bea he was the best man. He certainly was the smartest. He had a farm and he held down another job as well. The Wing men made jokes about him because he came from Iowa, from the big city of Des Moines. Even when he had learned almost as much about farming as they had, they still joked about him being an "outlander."

Saying that one day Uncle Jimmy was hoeing his leaf lettuce. Real fine lettuce that June, coming in green and fresh. And her papa, Jason Mills, standing looking at those pretty green leaves. Saying, "But when do they make a head of lettuce?" And Uncle Jimmy pausing and finally saying, "Late at night, city boy, late at night!"

They would laugh at her papa forever over that. Her papa might not have known about leaf lettuce back then, but he knew a lot about the world. He told Willie Bea about it. He would say why he looked so worried when he heard the *bulletins*. These were the new, brief warnings that came over the radio suddenly, any time of day or evening. They scared Willie Bea to death.

"Can't help to worry," her papa said. "Look at Japan's war with China last year. And Hitler, taking Austria and persecuting the Jews just this March 1938. Now he's taken over Czechoslovakia, with France and Great Britain lettin' him. You can bet Roosevelt is watching how Japan, Germany and that Italy are growing closer."

Willie Bea usually remembered everything her father told her, even when she didn't understand all of it. She knew if Hitler hated Jewish people first, he would hate Negro people like her whole family right after. There were all these Jewish people that Mr. Hitler had thrown out of Germany, her papa had told her.

Lazing under the back porch, Willie Bea idly ran her thoughts over her family. Her very own family included an older brother and sister, her sweet mama and her good papa, and Bay Brother—her little brother, who was Kingsley—and Bay Sister—her younger sister, who was Rhetta, but no one ever used those proper names. Her family was about perfect, so she didn't dwell on them. But no one, herself included, could understand how two farm folks like Uncle Jimmy and Aunt Lu could have such impossible children as Big and Little Wing.

Well, how someone like Aunt Lu could have a brat like Little Wing, Willie Bea thought. Her cousin Big wasn't really bad at all.

Carefully, now she crawled from under the porch. She was hardly aware she was moving.

6

Uncle Jimmy was silent, stubborn. He was full of himself, her mama said. Because Uncle Jimmy's farm was the biggest in the family. Because he had a truck, and a black touring car like Uncle Donald's. Uncle Donald was her mama's oldest brother.

"Oooh!" Willie Bea whispered. Her legs had fallen asleep and standing up straight was hard. She had to stamp her feet a moment to get them back to normal. Then she raced inside the house and up the bare brown stairs. She took the stairs two at a time. She stopped at the top. In the light of the window, she thought to look at her dress. It was red dotted Swiss, a pinafore with sleeves, tied like an apron behind her back. The front of it now showed dirt and streaks of green moss where she had lain and slid on her stomach under the rear porch.

"Oh, it's all dirty!" she sighed.

She wouldn't dare stand before her mama with her starched dress all soiled, or in front of relatives who had driven all the way from Ashtabula in their grand touring Ford motor car, Willie Bea thought. She sighed deeply.

Everyone in the family had a motor car except Willie Bea's family. Her father shunned automobiles, although her mother didn't mind them. Her papa had never been behind the steering of a motor car. Couldn't drive a lick. When the cousins teased Willie Bea about this, she had no good comeback. She was still trying to think of one.

Now she turned and jumped back down the stairs. She hurried to the kitchen to clean her dress. She took a dish towel and wet and soaped it with lye soap. Then she scrubbed her bodice as hard as she could. She rinsed the towel until all the soap was out. This she did over the washtub, using glasses of water from the water reservoir in the wood cookstove. The water in the deep holding tank in the stove stayed warm the whole day. She dipped the glass and filled it from the reservoir, poured it over the towel and wiped at her bodice. By the time she was through, the whole front of her dress was soaking wet.

But it's mostly clean! she thought happily. Maybe Mama won't notice. Gee whiz, I have to get going!

First she found a dry towel and blotted the wet part of her dress with it. The towel soaked up a good bit of the wetness.

When Willie Bea turned around to leave, she was not alone.

"Oh!" she nearly screamed, flinging herself back against the stove. And it was a good thing no fresh wood was burning inside it.

Before her stood Little Wing and her own Bay Sister, watching her. They were exactly the same height, but Little was twelve, as was Willie Bea. While Bay Sister looked so sweet in the face, Little Wing always had a frown and was plain ugly, was Willie Bea's opinion.

She tried not to look shocked to see them, although seeing them there so suddenly had scared her witless for a few seconds.

"Hey," Willie Bea said, as calmly as she could. "Want a drink of water?"

"Looks like you done drunk it all," said Little. "But seems you missed you mouth!"

"Shut up!" Willie Bea told her.

"But, Willie Bea, you got yourself all wet," Bay Sister said.

"Shoot!" cried Willie Bea. "Can't chall talk about nothin' else? What's goin' on over home?"

"Over home" was what everybody called the homestead that was Grand and Gramp Wing's home. Over home was the very first Wing house ever built.

"Mama and Grand and Aunt Mattie cookin' everythin'. We all eatin' over home and—" Bay Sister didn't get to finish. Little interrupted her.

"If they was anythin' goin' *on* over there, why you think we over here? Not to see you, anyway!" said Little.

"Then what're you doin' here?" Willie Bea asked. "Get on out, if not to see me."

"I had to help this baby chile get across the road," said Little. "She too afraid to cross it by herself. Sayin', 'Little, come help me. I'm afraid to fall in the ditch. Help me, Little, I'm so afraid.'"

"I never did," Bay Sister said. "You just followed me over here. I cross the road any time I want to."

"'Course she does," Willie Bea said. "Girl, you can sure lie."

"Who you callin' a lie?" said Little. She put both hands on her hips.

Little was swayback. She had on a white pinafore with pink piping along the hem and waist and the scalloped sleeves. When she stood leaning back like that, her stomach stuck out and the front hem of her dress was shorter than the back hem. Little's legs were more than slightly bowed.

She should never stand that way, Willie Bea thought. She giggled. She knew it wasn't nice to laugh at other people. But Little was such a nasty child, she thought. Who could help but believe she deserved having legs like that?

Swiftly, Willie Bea marched out of the kitchen, brushing by Little in the doorway and grabbing her sister's hand as she went. "Next time, you come home alone, don't be bringin' no *stranger*," she said to her sister. She pulled Bay Sister along.

"Better get out of this empty house, girl," Willie Bea called to the kitchen. She could tell Little hadn't yet thought to move. "Else somethin' get messed up, you'll be to blame."

"Gone tell my daddy on you, too," she heard Little say, coming through the dining room. "Callin' me a thief."

"Now, did I say thief? Tattle-tale!" Willie Bea said, stepping outside.

Little pushed her way out of the house and slammed the screen door behind her.

"*Oh, playmate*," Willie Bea began to sing, "*come out and play with me. And bring your dollies three. Climb up my apple tree . . .*"

"Big got your little brother, too," Little whispered in Willie Bea's ear. Willie Bea was hurrying across the yard with Bay Sister in tow. And Little was right behind her as close as she could get. "He took him downtown for some ice-cream," Little said. "Big and Hewitt Wing took you brother. And you know what that means!"

"*Slide down my rain barrel*," Willie Bea sang. She didn't even care whether she got the words right. "*Climb up my cellar door . . .*" She was about to die at the thought of Big and that halfwit Wing taking off with her baby brother. "*And we'll be jolly friends, forever more!*"

But she wasn't going to let Little know she was upset.

Have to get away from her and Bay Sis, too, she thought. Oh, yes, I know what it means, they took my baby brother for ice-cream. Ohhh! Big knows better! But I can catch them. I sure will. Know where they might be right now, if they're back from gettin' some ice-cream. Oh, that Big Wing. If I tell Mama, she'll kill him for sure! Should I? *'Should I may? Oh, should I may?'* That dumb song Toughy Clay had sung on her back porch came to her all of a sudden.

All at once Willie Bea thought to look around, to make sure Toughy wasn't hiding behind a tree somewhere. She didn't spot him. And she went on thinking about telling on Big and Hewitt.

Tell Mama right now, too, in front of everybody. Grinning, momentarily forgetting that her little brother could be in danger, she held Bay Sister's hand tightly. They were at the edge of the tar-and-gravel road that stuck to their feet.

Suddenly, the town siren blew. Today it was the Sunday siren. And tomorrow it would be the Monday siren. That was what her mama said. But all of the town kids called it simply The Whistle. The Whistle blew one long, loud scream for lunch. It blew three shortened blasts in case of fire. It blew hard and high for three minutes when there was a storm with a black tornado inside.

The siren filled Willie Bea's brain, along with the thought, *Now look both ways.* It was what Mama always told them. Patiently, Willie Bea looked up and down the road that went west to Dayton and east, veering north to

Springberg. There was nothing coming. They could see nothing, nor hear anything on the road.

Not one truck full of hogs, Willie Bea thought. And no motor car, little dot showin' through the dust, way off. But gettin' bigger. Until it 'most a black spot. Next, you hear it, huur-rum-rummmm, and it somebody goin' along just as fast and easy. Sweet mercy me! Willie Bea knew those words because her mama had a habit of saying "Sweet mercy me!" when something was too wonderful.

Gonna have me a motor car, too, come about 1944, Willie Bea thought. She figured that by the time she was eighteen, she should have the money for a *big* automobile like Uncle Jimmy's.

Now Willie Bea stood holding her sister's hand. The Whistle surrounded her thinking with a kind of piercing red heat. She let her thoughts dissolve as the heat came and went in three short blasts.

Fire. Somewhere, Willie Bea thought. She waited a moment, for fear the fire cars would come racing up the road. One time they'd come racing and run right over a hen and baby chickens that had been crossing. Little fuzzy yellow chickens. Splat. And for a week after, her cousin Big Wing would ask her every day when he saw her and each evening when he said goodbye and went home, "Why come them chickens have to cross the road? 'Cause they like to die—chicken pie!" And laugh his silly head off.

Nothin' comin' this way, Willie Bea thought. Be out toward Clifton Pike, by the sound of it. East. She knew her directions.

Over home, someone was holding open the screen and looking up and down the dusty road. Looked over at

Willie Bea and Bay Sister, gave a slight nod and went back inside. Someone was always watching out for the children. And Willie Bea knew it was now safe to cross the road.

Carefully, she picked her way across the tar and gravel. Some of the melted tar got between her toes. She didn't mind it. But Bay Sister did.

"It's dirty," she whimpered.

"I'll carry you, then," Willie Bea said, and swung her little sister up in her arms.

"Big baby!" a gruff voice said behind them. It was Little Wing, passing them by and sprinting to the old farmhouse that sat back a ways across the road. Over home.

"You *better* run," Willie Bea said.

"Blah-blah, dribble-mouth!" Little yelled. She turned and made an ugly face at them.

Willie Bea pretended unconcern. She knew this was no way for cousins to be acting. She concentrated on carrying her sister. Once they'd crossed the Dayton road, she set Bay Sister's feet gently in the sweet clover of Grand and Gramp Wing's big old bluegrass lawn.

2   Every homestead, every first house ever built for a people, a family, should look like Grand and Gramp Wing's farmhouse. That was Willie Bea's opinion. The house made her feel peaceful each time she walked up the wide stone steps. It wasn't an enormous house. In fact, it had the same number of rooms as her own house. But it was the way it seemed protected by Grand and Gramp's lawn that made it like a dream and, for her, the mark of country and family.

The lawn fanned out and down from the fieldstone porch clear to the Dayton road. It flowed around the house to the side, spreading out all along to a two-acre field where Grand had her garden. Almost every year about August, when the corn was good and high, Willie

Bea would think to borrow her dad's box Brownie camera and take a picture of Grand standing in front of her corn. "Corn be high as heaven," Grand would say, "and me, I'm on my way." Then she would laugh heartily at herself, posing with her pitchfork in one hand and her hoe in the other. Soon after that, they'd have sweet corn every day.

"What's the pitchfork for, Grand?" Willie Bea always asked when she took the picture of Grand. And Grand would say, "Hoe is for the row. Pitchfork for what might be hidin' deep in the dark of my tight corn rows."

"What could be hidin', Grand?" Willie Bea had thought to ask one time. And Grand had said, "The boogie man!" And that had nearly scared Willie Bea to death, and thrilled her at the same time. She did love scary thoughts.

When the picture was developed, there would be Grand looking tiny beneath her corn. That was the way it looked to Willie Bea, just as if Grand Wing had been standing *beneath* the high tassels. But most of the picture would be that lawn, spreading out in front of Grand and the corn. And Willie Bea wouldn't have dreamed she had taken so much of the grass. She hadn't meant to.

Oh, the grass! Willie Bea thought now. Her feet felt the coolness under the heat at the top. The grass was springy, was darkly fresh this late fall. There was still some shade around. And even where there was no shade, coolness seemed to flow under the ground and make the grass that rich green, that loving green of Grand and Gramp Wing's lawn.

In front of the fieldstone porch was a maple tree. Gramp had made a swing for her there.

Big old rope! Willie Bea thought. She had been with

Gramp when he gathered the new rope in his great hands and swung it up over the branch. Pulled it down to make the knot, and slid the knot up the rope to tighten it around the branch. He had a plank notched at each end. And he fixed the plank over the rope at the bottom to make a comfortable seat.

"Now," he'd said. "I made this swing for you, Willie Bea. Now you swing in it good."

And ever after, the swing was hers, although Big and Little and Hewitt, whenever he came to visit, claimed that Gramp had meant it for all of them. Said he'd only said it was hers because she was a little dummy you had to favor to keep her from crying. Willie Bea had punched each one of them for that lie, too.

It will always be my swing, she thought. Although now it was Bay Brother and Bay Sister who used the swing. Willie Bea also had an older brother and sister. They were Rebecca Esther Mills Knight and Jason Mills. But they were so much older, and married, that it was like they were somehow outside of Willie Bea's life. They had had a swing once, so they had told Willie Bea, on the same tree where hers was now. Perhaps they would come over to Grand's some time today. They usually did on one or two Sundays a month after church and with their families. So did Big and Little's older brother.

I'da seen them earlier if I'da gone to church this Sunday, Willie Bea thought. She leaned out over the railing of the porch to see around the corner of the house. There was the driveway. Full of motor cars!

There's Gramp's car and Uncle Donald's. And Uncle

Jimmy and Aunt Lu's. Aunt Lu drives it more than Uncle Jimmy.

They all called Uncle Jimmy "Uncle Speed" when he was behind the wheel of his motor car. That was how slow he went, like he was hardly moving. Of course, they didn't expect him to drive his hauling truck fast. Full of hogs on the way to Chillicothe and the hog market. Driving with her dad and Gramp, with Big along to help handle so many animals belonging to all three farms. They would take those southern Ohio hills slow and easy. Willie Bea wished sometimes that she was overgrown like Big so she could ride to the market in Chillicothe.

Ohhh! She glimpsed another car. It was almost pulled up behind the house, but she recognized the small part of it she could see. Red, and with the top down. It was Aunt Leah's car.

How'd she get up so early!

Aunt Leah lived over in Springberg. Had a beautiful dark brick house, with brown-and-yellow striped awnings all around. There was a cement birdbath on one side of Aunt Leah's house. Willie Bea couldn't get over that when she went to visit—a bitty bath for birds! And a great blue ball of a round mirror on a pedestal on the other side. Oh, Aunt Leah Wing was rich, Big said. And she was certainly beautiful. But Mama sniffed the air when people made a to-do over her younger sister. When the children were captivated by her fancy ways.

Because Aunt Leah's been married three times and not forty years old, Willie Bea thought, opening the screen door. And didn't stay unmarried long. That's why Mama sniffs, too.

Inside the house, there was an open staircase of oak to the second floor. The flooring was oak in every room. There was a pantry full of canned food Grand had put up. There were Heatrola stoves, one in the front room and one in the dining room. And a huge black cookstove in the kitchen. All winter long Gramp's house was warm, smelled of Grand's homemade potato-and-fish soup, homemade corn muffins, bread, doughnuts boiled in a great vat of lard. Willie Bea often lived here for weeks at a time in December and January, when she felt the cold most. But the cold never seemed to bother Bay Brother and Bay Sister in their own house across the road from over home.

"Hey," Willie Bea called out to no one in particular. She had to wait a minute for her eyes to adjust to the cool darkness of the house. Blinds halfway down over the screened windows. White lace curtains hanging limp. Bay Sister skipped straight through the house.

"Mama?" Willie Bea called. "Mama?"

Willie Bea could smell the odors of cooking on the still air. The fine smells made her mouth water.

"Willie Bea? In here, baby," came Marva Mills' voice. Then came surprised laughter, greetings from all the women as Bay Sister reached the kitchen.

Willie Bea could see now. Her eyes had adjusted. She was in a hurry, but she couldn't get by without saying hello to her uncles and Gramp sitting in the front room.

"Hey!" said Gramp. He sat comfortably in the big easy

chair by the window next to the radio. The radio had "The Church of the Air," Bishop Schrembs of Cleveland.

"Willie Bea." Gramps had on a gray suit. His big farmer hands and wrists seemed too large for the tight cuffs of his white dress shirt.

Oh, it was something, Willie Bea thought, Sunday time and company and Halloween begging time, all in one day and night!

She smiled. "Hey, Gramp," she said, going over to him. She gave her face for him to kiss. And delivered a good hug. Straightening up again, "Hi you, Uncle Donald?" Willie Bea said.

"Willie Bea," Uncle Donald said, shaking the ice in his highball glass. "Hey, you growin' too fast for me. Seems every time I come down, you done changed again." He had grown fatter in the face.

"Shoot, huh-unh," Willie Bea said, laughing. "Just my feet, maybe."

"Look to me you about as tall as Marva."

She leaned down, gave him a kiss. Uncle Donald smelled like cigars, although she didn't see one in his ashtray.

"Gone be real tall like Jason's people," said Gramp.

"Hey, Uncle Jimmy," Willie Bea had to say. For he was there in the rocking chair by the hallway to the dining room. She smiled as sweetly as she knew how, but she had never favored Uncle Jimmy.

Uncle Jimmy eyed her, nodded. There was no strong affection between them. She knew she could run inside Uncle Jimmy's house any time of the day to take a cold drink of water. She could sit in the kitchen watching Aunt Lu. Just resting, she would sit still until Aunt Lu offered her a cookie or an apple. It was like that in all houses of relatives. Any of the kids went in and out freely. Were watched over. Made to feel at home by aunts and uncles. But still, Uncle Jimmy's manner toward her and her little brother and sister was not as "close" as it could be.

Smiling, she edged politely through the front room. The men went back to their newspapers. Uncle Donald looked to have on a new suit, she noticed. Uncle Jimmy had on his usual blue worsted Sunday suit.

"Wouldn't you expect Jimmy always to wear blue?" her mama had said. "Lu can't do a thing with him. Nobody never could," she finished.

Too bad we didn't get to church, Willie Bea thought, loitering in the dining room. She touched the china on the long table. Felt the white lace tablecloth.

We didn't go 'cause Uncle Donald and Aunt Mattie Belle wouldn't feel up to it after their long drive to over home, Willie Bea thought. So her mama had said. Shoot. She had so wanted them all to go to church, even when most of the time she didn't much like going to church. She had gotten sassy with her mama about it. And her mama went to scold her for being smart. "Don't you abuse my word, Willie Bea," she had said, shaking her finger at Willie Bea. Her mama's face looked cross. "Don't you ever talk back to me!" And that was why Willie Bea had hidden herself under the wood rear porch in the first place. Angry at her mama. Hurt as she could be. She couldn't stand being scolded. Couldn't bear the shame she felt inside herself.

20

But all of us comin' into church like a whole reunion! she thought now. Wouldn't that be the best ole somethin'? And me and all my cousins on the front pew. Look how people see us and how well we dress, even in what Papa say is the worst times! I'm a *Mills* like my Papa. But Mama says I hold the style, I got the nerve and the stubborn streak of a Wing. Shoot. Mama.

Willie Bea had to hurry now and not let her mama know why.

"Willie Bea, baby," her mama said as Willie Bea came into the kitchen.

"Hey, Mama!" Willie Bea said. Her mother had her hands in the sink, snapping beans. There was a small pump mounted on the side of the basin. The water came running from the mouth of it whenever her mother pumped the handle. Then the cold well water gushed into a large colander. Already it was half full of beans, and the gushing water rinsed them.

Marva's anger at her daughter had evaporated. Willie Bea was so glad; she even forgot her hurry. Her mama was smiling over her shoulder at her. Willie Bea stood straighter.

Marva Mills had on her dotted Swiss dress, the one with the sailor collar of yellow to match the yellow french cuffs. The dress itself was brown with yellow polka dots. She was slim and had her hair marcelled in a perfect cascade of waves to her shoulders. She looked you straight in the eye and she never marred her bow mouth and her cheeks with anything more than a touch of rouge.

Next to her mother at the sink stood Grand Wing.

"Hey, hey, baby, Willie Bea!" she said. Grand's voice

was high and thin, like the tinkling bells in the snow at Christmas. Grand turned halfway around. She had been slicing peeled potatoes into a bowl of cold water. She wore a dark Sunday dress.

"Hey, Grand! Au gratin potatoes!" Willie Bea said.

"Yey!" said Grand. "You know it. No Sunday, fall, without my au gratin."

"Yes, ma'am!" said Willie Bea. Grand was small and neat; had on her black lace-up shoes that came up high, almost to her ankles.

"Commere, baby girl!" said Grand, wiping her hands on a dish towel.

Willie Bea was in her grandmother's arms. Letting herself be petted, pampered, her hair smoothed around her face. The ruffles of her bodice were pulled up through the fingers that were long, dark and tough, testing the amount of starch in the pinafore. Those sure hands knew their business of soothing and raising grandchildren.

Next Mattie Wing came forward. She had been rolling dough out with the rolling pin on the counter beneath the cabinets. She kept her floured hands away from Willie Bea's pretty dress.

"Uh-huh," she said. "You gettin' just too beautiful, chile. Marva, where she get her looks?"

"Me, who else?" said her mama. "Sweet, mercy me!" And the women laughed.

"Aunt Mattie, hey!" said Willie Bea, and was at once smothered against her aunt's bosom.

She remembered, suddenly, that she had to get out of the kitchen, out of the house. But she couldn't find a way to hurry Aunt Mattie Belle. Then she forgot again all about hurrying when her aunt commenced to whisper in her ear.

"Willie Bea, what kind is your favorite pie?"

"Huh?"

"What it is! Your favorite pie?"

"Pumpkin. Lemon meringue. Apple . . . I don't know!" whispered Willie Bea.

"Well, then, I'll make all three—how's that? Just for you!"

"Really, Aunt Mattie?"

"True, really," whispered Aunt Mattie Belle. "But you must pick me some more apples if I has to need some. Down in the cellar, bushels of good apples."

"Oooh, I sure will!" Willie Bea said, not bothering to whisper now.

Aunt Mattie released her. Willie Bea turned and probably would have reminded herself to leave the house by the back door if some movement hadn't caught her eye. By the table, across from the counter where Aunt Mattie Belle was carefully making her crusts for delicious pies. It was the breakfast table, round, walnut, made by Gramp long ago from his own mighty walnut tree. The table was shoved as far back in the corner as it would go. Soon it would hold cooling pies, baked corn, string beans, au gratin potatoes and sweet potatoes, all ready to serve in their proper courses. Later it would be cleared for the cousins to eat there.

Now the walnut table held a huge, shiny red pocketbook. The pocketbook was open. It had a silky black lining. A black lace hankie spilled from a zippered compartment. All around the bag on the table were pins for the hair, ribbons, a compact, lipstick and rouge. Combs. Everything about the red pocketbook was new and rich-looking.

Suddenly, someone flicked on the Tiffany lamp that hung over the table. And there was the one and only, the fine-as-wine Aunt Leah. Posed like a lady in the movie pictures, in a spotlight. She had Bay Sister on her lap. But it was Leah who was the only star. Her hair, marcelled and page-boyed to perfection.

"Look at me!" said Bay Sister to Willie Bea. "And I got Aunt Leah, too."

Each of them tried to get Aunt Leah for herself when-ever she came. Even the boys tried to stand in front of her and be polite, to see what kind of surprise she had brought, and for whom.

It was Willie Bea's turn for disappointment. Bay Sister had got to Aunt Leah first and had what Willie Bea might have got for herself. If only she had gone around to the back door instead of coming through the front room!

There was Bay Sister, Miss Rhetta Mills, with her hair piled on top of her head. She had pink bow ribbons on each side of the pile. Long, dangling earrings that sparkled in rainbows in the lamplight hung from her tiny ears. Around her neck was a velvet ribbon with a diamond clasp right in the middle. On her fingers were huge, sparkly rings.

"Oh, give me one?" said Willie Bea. She couldn't keep herself from begging. "Oh, please gimme me one of them rings?" But Bay Sister closed her hands tight and hid them under the table, shaking her head. She had on bright red lipstick. It made her mouth look beautiful, Willie Bea thought. And she had scarlet rouge on her cheeks.

"Now don't Bay Sis look like Clara Bow?" asked Aunt Leah.

"She look like she will be scrubbin' for a month," Willie Bea's mama said. She glanced over her shoulder, saw her child all made up and went back to work.

No point in asking Leah to do any cooking, the glance seemed to say. But it was a fact that Leah supplied the extra money so they all could have a fine Sunday dinner with all the trimmings and even come out ahead after. It was true, Leah was most generous. Any time any of the children needed a new dress or a new coat, she was willing to take care of it. She was a very decent spendthrift. But, oh, what they all had to put up with! Leah was a fortune teller, and that wasn't all.

Leah, exciting the children half to death. She sometimes plucked Bay Sister or Willie Bea right out of the yard and took them off to Springberg. Just snatched the babies and kept them for a day or two. Marva never knew what she did with them for two whole days. Leah had no children of her own. And back the kids would come after a day or two, with new dresses from the Penney's and lots of big ideas. Marva never knew with what-all Leah had filled the children's heads. With wanting what-all.

"You look so pretty, Aunt Leah," Willie Bea thought to say. She could not get her voice above a whisper. She was so disappointed. And knew for certain, no doubt about the route, that she had lost out to her baby sister.

Aunt Leah was looking gorgeous. She had on a full red

dress, cut low in a scalloped neck. It had side pockets and a shiny belt, like the skin of a snake. She had on silk stockings—Willie Bea could tell the smooth chiffon. And red pumps that shone in tiny diamond shapes, just like the snake belt.

"Willie Bea, you are growin', goodness. How old are you now?" asked Aunt Leah.

"Just twelve," said Willie Bea, "August nineteen."

"August nineteen," Aunt Leah mused. She uncrossed her long, slender legs and reached for the red pocketbook. "Me see," she said to herself. And, sighing, she searched until she found what she was looking for. *The Wizard of Odds and Even Almanac*, 1938 edition.

"Oooh!" sighed Willie Bea.

Everyone looked around to see. "Oh, Lord," said Willie Bea's mama, turning away.

"Whoo! Here we go," Grand said, and chuckled to herself.

"What she got?" Aunt Mattie asked Marva. If Aunt Mattie had been a Wing, she would have known right away. As it happened, she'd never come across anyone like Aunt Leah before marrying into the family.

"It's her vibrations book," said Marva. "You must've seen it once or twice."

"Her what?"

"Wait," said Marva.

Aunt Leah flipped through the book. "August nineteen," she said. Willie Bea let her hands rest on the table, trying not to seem nervous or excited.

"What's it say?" she whispered.

"Me see," said Aunt Leah. "Now, the waver back and

forth, that vibration is life. You know that. I tole you that before."

"Yes, ma'am," whispered Willie Bea.

Aunt Leah's starry, mascaraed eyes shone brightly. "Everything, from a grain of sand to the sun size, from the mackerel to the shark, from the big shot to the wino—"

"Leah, cut it," interrupted Willie Bea's mama.

"Come on, I didn't say nothin'—"

But again Marva Mills interrupted. "I said, cut out the grown-up business."

"From the mackerel to the shark," Aunt Leah repeated. She had Willie Bea and her sister's full attention. Willie Bea could hardly believe Aunt Leah's special magic would be directed at her alone.

"Every form of good, bad, breathing life on this round earth has a waver rate just particular to theyself. You see?" asked Leah.

Willie Bea and her sister nodded, fascinated, although they didn't understand a word of it. They knew food preparation was going on all around them in the busy kitchen. Still, they could not take their eyes from Aunt Leah's gorgeous face.

"All wavers be cause by the trinity of Freedom, Life and Love Thy Neighbor," continued Aunt Leah. "They got light, oh, and they got feelin's and they got voices, wavers has."

"Wavers, vibrations, do?" whispered Willie Bea.

Aunt Leah nodded. "And they can be shaped into numbers. Now." Leah licked a painted index finger and flipped over pages of her pamphlet.

"She believe that stuff, too," said Grand, placing her au

gratin potatoes atop the stove, all ready to bake in the oven. Willie Bea spied candied sweet potatoes waiting atop the stove, too. All the time she worked, Grand Wing chuckled.

"Wish you wouldn't encourage Leah, Mama," said Marva to Grand.

"Ain't my place, encourage or discourage," Grand answered her daughter, the one she thought of always as the serious, sensible one. "My place to listen and unnerstan'."

"Hunh," said Marva, and kept her peace.

Aunt Leah studied her book. "It's a fact, we each has numbers," she said. "Everything be touched by the special number it has. And there are numbers for each name, each activity, each day and month of each year. Combinations be for certain months and the dates on which they most often appear. Now."

She flipped more pages. "We look for the Fast numbers first. They the ones appear more than the Law of Averages rating, which come three or four times a year. Now."

Leah looked up and down the pages. "This book don't have no Willie listed for ladies. But it has Bea—Beatrix or Beatric. Marva, what her full Bea name?" she asked Willie Bea's mama.

"Lord," Marva muttered.

"It's Willie Bea*trime*," said Willie Bea.

"Bea*trime?* Well then, we'll say it's close to Beatric," her Aunt Leah said. "We'll use the numbers for Beatric and say it Beatrime. Now. Beatrime is two-eight-three and one-eight-three. That's all right. It might work out. Number one-eight-three appear three times in the month of August. Not bad. And two-eight-three appear once. Now.

Let's take your name. Beatrime Mills. Now, I happen to know what numbers stand for what letter of the alphabet. Like, A, J and S are all number one. And I and R are both number nine. Beatrime, your first name comes out to two-five-one-two-nine-nine-four-five. Add the numbers across, they make thirty-seven. Your last name is four-nine-three-three-one. Add it, it come to twenty. And thirty-seven plus twenty gives fifty-seven. Add five, seven, gives twelve. Add one, two, gives three. Number three is Beatrime Mills' *vital number*. Number one-two-three is your *lucky number* combination. Add one, two, three across, they are six, one half of number twelve. Now, remember Beatrime is two-eight-three and one-eight-three?"

"Yes," whispered Willie Bea. The kitchen was utterly quiet. Even Marva Mills had stopped her work at the sink to listen. She lifted the colander, full of beans now, and quietly placed it on an old work table.

"Number one-eight-three," said Leah. "Adds up to one plus eight plus three, gives *twelve*. Remember thirty-seven plus twenty gives fifty-seven?"

Willie Bea managed a nod.

"Five plus seven gives *twelve*," said Leah triumphantly.

"What about two-eight-three?" said Marva. She had turned all the way around from the sink now. She held her head high and would not let go of Leah's eyes.

"Hunh?" said Leah.

"I said, what about *two*-eight-three? It never add up to twelve." Marva stood still, tall, most serious in her dotted Swiss.

A silence, in which the two sisters regarded each other.

Willie Bea looked solemnly from one to the other. She had seen her mama and her aunt in fights before.

"Two-eight-three," murmured Aunt Leah. "Two plus eight plus three gives thirteen."

"Thirteen," said Marva quietly, "not twelve." She looked at Willie Bea.

"Thirteen is one plus three," Leah murmured again. "Equals four. Four into twelve equals . . ." She paused, waiting.

"Three!" sang Willie Bea, swinging from side to side. She felt like jumping up and down. "Three! Three!"

"Three," said starry-eyed Aunt Leah. "It work out 'most always. Three. Bea*trime* Mills' vital number!"

Marva Mills knew there was something wrong with the numbers. There was a trick to it somewhere. Every time Leah did the numerology, Marva knew there must be something *wrong* in it. But never did she have the time to ponder or figure out what that could be. Now she held her peace. She went about getting her pole beans ready for this Sunday afternoon dinner at which all the Wing families would break bread together. Renew the ties that bind.

Just then they heard the screen door open in the front. Voices. In came Aunt Lu Wing, followed by Uncle Jimmy carrying a huge roaster. He musta gone home after Aunt Lu, Willie Bea thought. So busy talkin', didn't hear a car.

"Turkey!" shouted Bay Sister.

"I'll be darn!" said Willie Bea. "It is! No chicken this Halloween."

"Well, hi, yall," said Aunt Lu. "Lordy, that hot cookstove. Had to put the turkey in, the middle of the night, almost. Get it done for now. What time was it I put it in, Jimmy? Five, six? Jimmy know." Uncle Jimmy said not a word. He seldom did when Aunt Lu went on. "It'll stay hot in the roaster, Grand Wing," she said, "if you just keep it atop the cookstove. Be room? Hey, chile?" she said to Bay Sister.

She spoke a warm greeting to Aunt Leah. She smiled on Willie Bea. Then grinned. "Hey!" she whispered loudly at Willie Bea. "How it go—'An all us other childern, when the supper things is done, We set around the kitchen fire an' has the mostest fun . . .'"

"'. . . A-list'nin' to the witch-tales 'at Annie tells about.'" Willie Bea promptly took up the next line of the James Whitcomb Riley poem, "'An' the Gobble-uns 'at gits you Ef You Don't Watch Out!'" It was her favorite poem any time of year.

"Yes! 'Little Orphant Annie,' yes!" laughed sweet Aunt Lu. "But it ain't Halloween yet, darlin'."

"Well, it's the night for beggars," Willie Bea told her. "And we'll be by to see you, Aunt Lu. We'll be all in costume, too."

"Well, for . . . And me with no popcorn nor candy! Wonder why Little didn't say nothin' about it? I'll have to hurry, after supper, too."

"Yes, ma'am," Willie Bea said politely, glad she had reminded Aunt Lu.

Aunt Lu continued her busy swing around the room. "Mattie Belle? Honey, hush! I know you tired. All that long way! Get off you feet, I'll finish it up." Aunt Lu had on a sheer apron over an organdy dress she'd made herself.

Aunt Mattie Belle groped protectively for her pies.

They all knew Aunt Lu, sweet as she was, could do no more than wreck a decent pie.

"She try too hard about they crusts," Grand always said about Aunt Lu. "She work and work at the dough until she turn it to paste. Nerves."

"You'd have nerves, too, if Big and Little was yours," Willie Bea's mama had said.

All at once her mama jumped a foot in front of where she had been standing. Her eyes looked wild. She clapped her hands over her ears. She spun around, wide-eyed, looking half-crazed about the room.

Lookin' like a witch, a goblin, Willie Bea thought, and felt a chill up her spine.

"Marva?" said Grand.

"Shhh!" Marva said. She rushed out of the kitchen into the dining room, into the front room. She rushed upstairs. They could hear her come directly over their heads. She came back down and into the kitchen.

"Where!" she said to Willie Bea. Stamping her foot. "Where is he? Where's Bay Brother!"

Willie Bea sucked in her breath. "Ohhhh!" she moaned at last, remembering what she had forgotten. Her baby brother. And Little Wing was gone, too.

Both she and her mama were at the back door, tripping over each other to get outside first. It was Marva's hand that went right through the screen, as if she had not realized the screen door was there. But that didn't stop her. She carefully pulled her hand out of the torn screen and went on her way.

Aunt Lu was behind them, whining. She took the door by the handle, as though to come outside. But, turning away, she went back in the kitchen, calling for her husband.

"Oh, Lordy," they could hear her. "Oh, Jimmy, come fix it. *Fix* it!" She wasn't talking about Grand's screen door, either, Willie Bea realized. "It's Big again," Aunt Lu cried. "I know it is."

Of course, she was right, too.

"Jimmy! Jimmy! Big's done it again!"

**3** Willie Bea had a hard time keeping up. Her mama cut across the lawn and through that part of the land where Grand had grown her corn. Now all of the corn was cut down. Corn was being cut on farms all around. On bigger stretches of land than Grand Wing's bitty plot. Way in the night, every night this week, Willie Bea had heard tractors humming and hauling, in a hurry to get the harvest finished during dry days. Wouldn't do for the farm machines to sink in the muddy, soaking-rain fields of November. And Willie Bea knew that farmers of the land would work clear to dawn if they had to.

The sharp spikes of cut cornstalks stuck out of Grand's harvested land. Willie Bea's mama didn't seem to notice them. She had taken off her high heels and rolled her stockings down and over her toes. She had wadded her chiffon stockings, worn only on Sundays, and flung them onto the grass at the edge of Grand's corn plot. Then she had flung her high-heel pumps onto the lawn. She was barefoot now, just like Willie Bea.

In her hurry, Marva stepped too near a corn spike and it creased her ankle, leaving a white line against her brown skin. This happened more than once.

"Ouch! Ouch!" Marva whispered, through the plot of spikes. White stripes soon criss-crossed her ankles, but she did not slow down.

Willie Bea knew exactly how being stuck and scratched by a corn spike felt.

Give you that icy feeling all inside, she thought as she hurried, following her mother. That was what she called it, "that icy feeling." She had a few spike scratches now, herself. And when it happened, it hurt so, all of a sudden, that the pain of the scratch streaked up through her like a painful, icy cold.

"Mama, slow down!" Willie Bea hollered. But her mama would not slow down.

Shoot! thought Willie Bea. Mama been runnin' through places all her born days, but I been doin' it just a little while.

Her mama kept going and Willie Bea kept on following. They headed diagonally across the wide field belonging to Uncle Jimmy and Aunt Lu. The field had been harvested the week before and was full of corn shocks. These were stacks of cut cornstalks tied around the middle with heavy twine and set up to dry. The corn shocks were full of mice inside, getting at the corn and fodder. Willie Bea never knew whether the mice or sudden breezes caused the shocks to tremble. They did rustle so. The shocks looked to her like fat ladies in long yellow dresses. And with tight sashes around their waists. All over the field, the ladies stood like dancers at a ball, frozen still as the music stopped.

On the ground at the base of the corn shocks were huge field pumpkins, many of them still on the vine. Some of them weighed fifty pounds or more. Uncle Jimmy had such a crop of pumpkins this year, he couldn't sell them all, Willie Bea's papa had told her. And what was left of the pumpkins by the final days of the Halloween month, any of the Wing families could have.

Big ole pumpkins! Willie Bea thought, racing by. Her papa had taken a couple home to carve and put candles inside. Tonight Willie Bea would light them.

She did so love to see jack-o'-lanterns grinning with their flickering lights on front porches all over town. Most of the carved pumpkins came from this one field of Uncle Jimmy's. And that made Willie Bea feel so proud.

Her mama did slow down a moment as they came around a corn shock toward the back of Uncle Jimmy's house. A low, barbed-wire fence separated the backyard of Uncle Jimmy's house from the field. A path led right up to the fence. There the path disappeared, then reappeared again on the other side of the fence. The path had been made by Willie Bea's and Big and Little's older brothers and sisters, she supposed. Now Willie Bea and Big and Little and her little brother and sister kept up the path, walking back and forth, trotting, running between the two houses. They would climb over the fence and pick up the path again on the other side.

Panting, Willie Bea caught up with her mama.

"Not there," Marva murmured, looking at the back of the house. You could always tell when a house was empty. No sound. Nobody flying around, busy. Even the chickens in the chicken coop were quiet in the shade. Willie Bea regarded the old chickenhouse with its tin roof. She and Big and Little often slept all night on the slant of the cool roof under the stars. Everyone marveled that they could stay asleep there through a starry night and not slide off. They never did slide off. They were experts at sleeping on a slant. Only one thing could get them off the roof in the night, and that was rain and wind in their faces. Willie Bea noted Big and Little's homemade stilts just like her own, leaning against the chickenhouse. They must have been stilting for Cousin Hewitt.

Marva Mills was moving again, fast. Her bare feet made light puffs of sound as they padded over the dark earth. Willie Bea stayed beside her. She could hear her mama's breath coming in sighs from her chest. But her mama was not panting, not yet. She was breathing hard and deep for strength. Marva Mills was strong and country-smart. She knew her way through the fields and into the wood that also belonged to Uncle Jimmy.

Say that some gentleman came along one day and offered Uncle Jimmy a fortune for his wood, twenty-five hundred dollars, Willie Bea remembered now as they hurried along.

Uncle Jimmy had laughed in the man's face. He believed his wood was worth a fortune because he would believe anything anybody told him. But he was no fool. He would not take the fortune for his woodland, whose very shade was worth more than anything Uncle Jimmy could think to name.

They were in the wood. It was a thick growth of trees, stands of oak and elm and great old walnut trees. It went on and on clear to the far side of town. You could find strangers wandering through it most times. You could find hoboes resting off the roads, living awhile from the berries and nut trees. Uncle Jimmy tolerated all kinds of strangers, for these were hard times. But strangers must never take an axe to a tree. There were signs posted everywhere. "WARNING. HIM DARE CUT DOWN, BE WARE." Those who knew Uncle Jimmy knew he wasn't about to hurt anybody, although he carried a shotgun when he walked his wood. And those who didn't know him, had never heard of him and came upon a sign, could not be sure. They were trespassers, after all. And it was another man's wood.

"They'll be in the clearing," Marva whispered, moving fast along an almost invisible path carpeted with leaves. Trees were bare and their tall, twisting branches were cut-out shapes against the bright sky.

"Mama," said Willie Bea. "He won't mean it bad, Big won't."

"No? No?" whispered her mama. "That's what they all say. That's what they all tell me. But it's not their child he does it to. It's not their baby!"

"Big hasn't hurt Bay Brother yet."

"Yet!" her mama said in a strangled voice. "My Lord, and he so overgrown and about half-witted, too!"

"He's not half-witted, Mama. Not like half-wit Hewitt, Big's not."

"Hewitt's no dummy," her mama said, her breath rushing in a whisper. "He gets the best kind of grades in school, Mattie Bell tells me."

"That don't make him smart," Willie Bea said. "That just makes him the teacher's pet. Aunt Lu says Big is just overgrown. He grew too fast. Who ever hear of a thirteen-year-old over six feet tall and weighing two hundred pounds, Aunt Lu says," said Willie Bea. "And Big not knowing what to do with all that weight, all that heighth. Sometimes he sits all day on a straight chair, for fear if he moves, he'll turn over a table or knock Aunt Lu's glass figurines and shatter them."

"Shhhh!" her mother warned. "They hear us and Big might make a mistake."

Willie Bea shut up. But she didn't think Big was bad or mean, the way Little was. Or namby-pamby, the way Hewitt was. Big couldn't help himself. He was just so awfully *big*. When he got hold of an idea, it was like he was too big for the idea to get to his head. It would seem to simply sit well with him somewhere below his mind for a month of Sundays. And it would take strong talking by some grown-up, usually, to make him let it go.

They went silently. It was necessary to leave the path and the dry leaves that crackled as they stepped on them.

Wood is not like any other place, thought Willie Bea, mindful of tree and trunk, bark and leaf. Somethin', the way all of it so quiet. Not because you come walk in it, but because it's wood's way. All still. All itself of silence.

Now, as they moved swiftly along, it came to Willie Bea how to go silently, how to keep her feet from making sound. How to feel wood and be a part of it, almost the way the sunlight and shade, the sound of birds, was a part of it.

Her mama picked their way. Leading, her mama's small, neat self swayed rhythmically in her Sunday dress. Thoughts, memories popped into Willie Bea's head.

Her mama telling, "I went to college. Just one year, though. Hunh! Oh, how I loved it! Wilberforce. I had one dress for Sunday and one dress for the week."

"Just one same dress a week!" Willie Bea had said, surprised as she could be.

"Uh-hunh," her mama said. "Every night I'd wash and iron that week-dress. Iron it dry. But it was hard way, havin' but one dress for every day. I sang in the choir. Oh, we had a fine choir there. I took Latin and history. History! I took art and could draw fairly well. Hunh. I quit 'cause of that one week-dress, mostly. It shamed me. I should have been bigger than that, but I was just an ole girl, wanting pretty things."

"That don't seem wrong to me," Willie Bea had said.

"Had no money," her mama explained. "Uncle Jimmy had to go to school, and he worked and helped me and helped himself. He finished. He went to Antioch College. Uncle Jimmy is a college grad-u-ate, like your father."

He don't act like he been to college atall, Willie Bea thought now, about Uncle Jimmy. And then it came to her that maybe you could go to college and it couldn't touch you. College had touched her papa and her mama. But it had never touched Uncle Jimmy. It didn't make him different, she thought, watching the smooth sway of her mama's walk in one of the more than a few dresses she owned now. It didn't forever change him like it must have her mama and papa. They were so very much different from everyone else in the family.

How different? Willie Bea wondered. Gentler. Kinder. And smarter, she thought. College did all that!

Then she and her mama were there. A clearing was suddenly opening, like a pouring, a draining of light and space into a large rectangle in the wood. Like a broad, bright box. It was a weedy place, full of stillness. There were wild flowers sprinkled everywhere. Pretty yellows and blues. A very few white daisies were fading away as the fall inched toward its end. Wild flowers would grow clear on through fall almost to the first snow of November, as long as there was no frost on the pumpkins.

Big and Hewitt were there, as Marva and Willie Bea had known they would be. And Little was there, as Willie Bea had suspected she would be. Willie Bea and her mama stood among the trunks of close trees. They would not move for fear of scaring Big. He was in the middle of a shot. He stood there, aiming. Hewitt sat on the ground beside Big. Little sat next to him. Her legs were crossed and she chewed on a stalk of weed. She and Hewitt stayed very still, so as not to disturb Big's aim.

About thirty-five feet in front of Big and Hewitt, almost in the middle of the clearing, sat Willie Bea's baby brother; her mama's youngest son, Kingsley, called Bay Brother.

Marva gave a tiny gasp. It was so soft, Willie Bea barely heard it. Still and all, it was a sharp, sad cry. Willie Bea's heart went out to her mama and to her baby brother. If she could have kept her mama from seeing, she would have. It was her job to watch out for Bay Brother. She always did. That is, except for this one time and maybe one or two other times this year since Big had gotten his equipment for Christmas.

But Bay Brother did look slightly the worse for wear to Willie Bea. His short pants were soaked through with vanilla ice-cream, as was his Sunday shirt. Marva had made it herself, out of fancy shirting, too. Bay Brother held in his tiny hands a carton of homemade ice-cream. You could buy it right downtown at the grocery. Newby Bishop, the grocer, made it himself. Big had stopped long enough at Uncle Jimmy's house to get a wood spoon for Bay to eat with. And now the baby was eating directly from the carton. Sitting there on the ground. And the ice-cream melted out of the bottom almost as fast as Bay could dip his spoon in to spoon it out. He was having the best time, though, Willie Bea could tell.

In his seventh heaven, she thought. Look at him. He gettin' about half of it and losin' half of it, it's meltin' so.

Surrounding Bay Brother on the ground were broken pumpkins. Small ones. Big must have plucked them right from the vine and kept them in a cool, dark place, like Uncle Jimmy's cellar, until he had enough for practice. One little pumpkin had been placed on Bay Brother's head. Then, another, and another.

Bay was not upset by the pumpkin shoot, or, at least, Big snatching him away and buying him ice-cream. And he could eat out of a pint carton, with an out-sized wooden spoon and not move his head a quarter of an inch from the perfect straight-on position in which Big had posed it. Big had quietly warned Bay not to move. And Bay obeyed. He was too young to be afraid. He probably didn't feel a thing and never would feel a shot. But then it was happening.

It happened so fast. Willie Bea was aware of sound, like something gathering air to it and carrying it along at high speed. She had seen Big pull back the string of his great bow. Somehow, she had missed seeing the arrow that he pulled with the string. She saw Big's fingers move. She had a fleeting thought: Why in the world would Uncle Jimmy buy Big that great bow with some arrows! She thought she heard the bowstring vibrate. She heard that heavy-sounding rush of air.

The sunlight and space of the clearing seemed to explode. The pumpkin atop Bay's head burst into pieces, dripping seeds. A few seeds fell on Bay Brother; most exploded behind him. Casually, he let the spoon drop, reached into the carton with his hands and came up with three fingers full of melted ice-cream. Which he managed to slurp into his mouth. Without moving his head a bit.

Well trained! Willie Bea thought.

The moment Bay Brother caught sight of his mama was the second Marva Mills made her move. She tore a whip of a tree out of the ground. Grunting, she snatched it from the soft earth. It had a bunch of dead leaves still clinging to the top of it, was young and green. She broke it in half across her knee. And tore the sinewy skin clean away. All this done in a very few motions and in the time it took Bay Brother to shout.

"Mama! Hey! . . . Nook-a Big gimme. See? . . . Ice-keem!"

Big spun around just as Marva Mills stepped high, as though she meant to climb a hill. She was there, the worst kind of surprise out of nowhere.

Big's eyes grew huge and frightened. His dark yellow skin blanched pale as Marva Mills struck his jaw with her open palm. She had to jump to do it. The sound of that smack was like a gunshot in the still clearing.

Willie Bea witnessed the scene as from a dream. She watched, stunned, as Big dropped to one knee, holding his jaw. He squeezed his eyes shut and bowed his head. She saw Little Wing and Hewitt Wing seem to rise slowly from the ground in one rhythm and slide away, as if pulled by the same invisible string. She saw Big's face break up in pieces as tears filled his eyes. She knew the smack from her mama could never hurt big old Big. What had broken him down was his pride. His shame at having done something so terribly wrong. He knew it was wrong, but it was like he never thought about that until the very moment he was caught. And then having to be brought up short by his aunt, whom he loved dearly.

*Like to die, chicken pie!* crossed Willie Bea's mind.

She was in the clearing beside her mama. And she hadn't realized she had moved. She saw her mama make a fist, give Big a bop on the very top of his head.

Willie Bea grabbed her mama's wrist. It was like she somehow had got hold of it and didn't know when she had done so.

"Don't," she said to her mama.

Her mama was panting. "Well, I know I mustn't," Marva whispered. "But, Big, you are so . . . so . . . wrong! So stupid! How could you? You could miss and shoot him through the eyes! My baby!" She took the switch she was holding and snapped it across Big's hands. That had to sting. And Big quickly put his hands behind him.

"Don't!" Willie Bea told her mama. But Marva Mills simply marched around Big, whipping his hands as he scooted about, trying to get away from her. When Big finally got to his feet, backing away from his aunt, Willie Bea managed to snatch the switch away.

"Don't!" she said again. And her mama stood there a moment, exhausted and half ashamed at losing her temper.

"You deserved it," she told her nephew. "And I'm going to tell Jimmy, and don't you dare take Kingsley out of my sight again. You hear me?"

Big nodded.

"Say it. Say you won't," Marva said.

Big commenced backing away.

"Oh. Oh," Marva said, and tried to take the switch away from Willie Bea. But Willie Bea wouldn't give it up.

Big broke and ran. So did Little and Hewitt. They all three ran in three different directions. Marva Mills was left empty-handed. That was when she remembered why she was there in the wood. She went over and grabbed Bay Brother by his arm. She dragged him off behind her.

"The very idea!" she muttered furiously. Bay's carton of ice-cream was left in her wake. That caused Bay to wail a long, pitiful cry. But Marva didn't stop. She hurried from the clearing, talking a mile a minute. "Look at you!" she told her son. "Wait till I get you home. The idea! Jimmy's goin' to do somethin' with that boy—what boy? He's an overgrown, simple-headed dummy!" Bay Brother's feet barely touched the ground as she swung him along behind her. He wailed and wailed.

Willie Bea went over to recover Bay's ice-cream. She looked in the carton only to find that the ice-cream had melted away on the ground. She took up the carton and flung it into the high weeds and young saplings at the edge of the clearing.

She looked up to see Little staring at her from behind a tree. Willie Bea was so surprised, for a second she couldn't move. But she swiftly regained her senses. And carefully raised the switch she still held in her hand. "How 'bout it, Little?" she said. "You always want what someone else has."

She closed in on Little. "You're a one, just ten times worse than Big. I know it's you who reminds Big to use my brother. I know Big would never think of it if you didn't worry him. You're the worse one."

"You another one!" Little yelled and ran.

Willie Bea thought about chasing her cousin.

Nope, she thought. Don't want to muss up my pinafore chasing someone as bratty as Little, too. Take more than that child to make me spoil my looks.

Primly, she stood there in the clearing, cooling her anger. She touched her nicely fixed hair. Best hair-do done by Honey Clay, too. Don't let my head get sweaty, she thought. Don't let my curls go back home before I do!

Then she walked swiftly away. There was a nice coolness in the wood now, and Willie Bea could skip and not get hot. She thought she might be able to catch up with her mama, but she didn't know for sure. When soon she cleared the wood, she could see her mama almost halfway across Uncle Jimmy's field. Willie Bea glanced over at Uncle Jimmy's house. But Big and Little and that half-wit Hewitt were nowhere to be seen.

She could tell her mama was heading for home to clean up Bay Brother before the Sunday supper. Then, of course, she would have a word with Uncle Jimmy. Willie Bea could see it now. Her mama shaking her finger, and Uncle Jimmy, his head cocked to one side, looking sheepish and not facing her mama straight on. And then Big would get it from his own papa in the woodshed.

But it was Little that should get the whipping, Willie Bea knew. They always pickin' on Big 'cause he's so big, Willie Bea thought. She pushed out of her mind the fact that Big had lured her little brother into the wood to target-shoot. She knew that most of the time, when Big was mean, Little or others were the cause of his seeming to be mean. But she had a soft spot inside for her cousin Big.

*Hope to die, chicken pie!* Willie Bea knew what her mama would never understand about Big, even if she were to know. It wasn't easy for Willie Bea to put into words.

That Big could not miss with his great bow and arrow. That he would never take a chance with Bay Brother. There were no odds. He never missed. Big just had to shoot. It wasn't any practice. He knew how to shoot perfectly, just as Willie Bea knew how to walk the high crossbeam up in Uncle Jimmy's barn.

She and Little. It was their most favorite, dangerous game. They walked the three-inch-wide cross-beam *blindfolded*. Up there, she and Little were never at war. High up, where the sharp hay-mound odor stung their nostrils, they were not enemies, not brave, not even cousins. They were highly skilled. They did what they must. They kept the walk secret, knowing that grown-ups would not understand. But they could not stumble and fall. It never entered their minds they might.

She saw her mama weave around the corn shocks and orange-yellow pumpkins with Bay Brother flying and wailing behind her. Once through the field, her mama paused long enough to retrieve her stockings and high heels. Then she continued on.

Huh! This turnin' into some old Halloween, Willie Bea thought.

Be *careful*, she warned herself.

She watched as Marva Mills hurried her youngest son across the Dayton road.

Or the Gobble-uns might get *me*.

Willie Bea trotted over to Grand and Gramp's good house.

Gobble-un already got Bay Brother!

**4** It was some daytime, fall time, Halloween time. Willie Bea was sure she had never known a day quite like it. One minute, she would be hot and sweating; the next, she would be cool all over—her feet, yellowish-cold in the grass; her scalp under her hair-do, almost cold. That was when she knew the daytime had changed. The early Sunday coolish sunshine seemed to have flowed away. What she had now around her in the trees and up from the ground was that fall coolness that she knew would not go away again.

It'll stay cool this time, she thought. Indian Summer is all gone for good and true, I bet. Bet tonight'll be real chilly out. I'll make Bay and Bay Sister wear some sleeves. Me see—think I'll make them ghosty in sheets. Powder their faces and they won't need some masks. Papa can't buy us masks like that.

She was resigned to the fact that her papa had said no, he could not buy her and her brother and sister Halloween costumes.

"No *flatter* money again this year, Willie Beatrime," he told her. His eyes were twinkling at her, the way they would when he was sorry he had to hurt her, when he wanted to make light and cause her less pain. She had sure wanted a costume. Little had a costume. Big shunned costumes. But he did wear his rubber hip boots for cleaning outhouses. "I'm the giant Big," he'd said, the first time he wore the hip boots out of the catalogue, which said they were for fishing. Then he'd said, "I'm the giant Big" a million times, to anyone. It got a laugh the first time. Then it got tiresome.

They make you buy the whole costume, Willie Bea reminded herself, and a pirate suit may cost eighty-nine cent. And a girl's four-piece Spanish Costume In Brilliant Colors cost you another fifty cent. That's a dollar for me and Bay Sis and eighty-nine cent for Bay Brother. Dollar eighty-nine. And all us need new pajamas for the winter, made of flannelette, too. And they are sixty-nine cent a piece, too. Saw it all at the Kresge's store downtown. Remind Papa about the flannelettes. But he won't forget. Not for us, he won't, my papa!

Willie Bea squinted up at the sky. It seemed to have suddenly decided to grow gray clouds over the horizon.

Can't believe it's goin' to snow-shower this soon. No, don't let it do that! she thought. I can't stand that tonight, oooh!

But even as she watched, the clouds fell apart and formed and reformed. There was no steadiness or certainty about them at all.

Good, she thought. Maybe the night'll be clear for begging. I can take Papa's flashlight, if I have to. Maybe somebody'll build some bonfires to light the way.

Occasionally, some farmer would think to make a fire for the kids passing along the roads and fields.

Willie Bea sat on the lower step of Gramp Wing's front porch. She was waiting for three o'clock. That was the time when she would see her papa. She had waited as long as she could in Grand's kitchen. Little, Big and Hewitt were nowhere to be found. And Willie Bea didn't feel like looking for them.

Her mama had come back by herself afterwhile. Willie Bea knew then that her little brother must be taking a nap. For there was no one at home to watch him. Her mama never left him alone even for a minute when he was awake. But when he was asleep, he wouldn't awake again for at least an hour. Chap loved to sleep some sleep, she knew.

Her mama had come in the front door of Gramp Wing's house and had not gone to the kitchen. She was in the front room with the men, with Uncle Jimmy. She told Uncle Jimmy good.

Everyone in the kitchen had stayed quiet. Aunt Lu stretched her neck and stared at the back door, but she was listening, too. Willie Bea had seen Aunt Lu stretch like that countless times. And each time she was sure her aunt looked more and more like a turtle.

Lost its shell, Willie Bea thought, sitting on the step of Gramp's porch.

Aunt Lu wouldn't interfere with her husband's sister Marva Mills. Who would? Not even the men would. Least of all, Uncle Jimmy. Only Willie Bea's papa could get her quiet once she was "on a roll," as he called her spitfire anger at something.

Her mama's voice had been not so much loud as it was soft-edged, and hard and strong everywhere else but the edge of it.

"Jimmy, Jimmy," Marva Mills began. "Put down that paper, Jimmy. You know what I'm here for. Lu called you when I went out the back door. Why come you didn't come after us? Stop that boy of yours from doing what he was doing in the wood?"

They had heard Uncle Jimmy's paper when his sister Marva snatched it from his hands. "I'm talkin' to you!"

They all had known what Uncle Jimmy's expression would be. Hangdog. Big was just like him. You tell him he's wrong, he then knew it and hung his head.

Aunt Leah was there in the kitchen, still at the table, with Bay Sister, all dressed up, on her lap. Leah hadn't been looking at anything in particular. She had her arms around Bay Sister's waist, holding her tight. She had snuggled Bay Sister's neck. One of the sparkling earrings Bay Sister wore hung down the bridge of Aunt Leah's nose. Willie Bea had seen everything. Grand was there in the kitchen, and Aunt Mattie Belle. Aunt Mattie had held a sliver of apple pie before Willie Bea's mouth. Willie Bea had opened her mouth and gobbled the delicious, almost hot pie. Aunt Mattie gave Bay Sis a piece, too. It paid to stay close in a Sunday company kitchen. All movement and offering done in silence so they could listen to what went on in the front room. Grand had sighed heavily, but she would not get in the middle of a hot discussion between two of her children. They had all heard as much as they could, from the front room.

Willie Bea had heard quite a lot.

"He had pumpkins on my baby's head," she heard her mama say, in the front room. There was fury under the calm sound of Marva Mills' voice. "He stole the child away from here! Big took my child *down*town and bought him a pint of ice-cream. Probably *rode* Bay on the handlebars of his bike. And if that's not dangerous enough—"

"I tole him a hunnerd times not to do it no more," Uncle Jimmy interrupted.

"*Telling's* not enough," Sister Marva said. "Telling don't do doodly-squat!"

"Then Big takes my baby to the *wood*," they heard her say. "Way in the *wood!* And all kinds of hoboes and bums travelin' the roadways and restin' in there."

"Now. Now. I keep a good watch on my wood. You know—"

"Shut up, Jimmy. We all know you catch stray men in there, you fine them, tellin' them if they don't pay, you'll take them to the sheriff. If they got but a penny, a few cents, you take it. That's why you didn't stop Big. There wasn't any money in it. You don't do anythin' won't turn a profit! You make me sick!"

"Big. Big! Come in here!" Promptly, Jimmy Wing made an effort to put things right.

"You know perfectly well, Jimmy, Big's nowhere in this house," Marva said.

"Now, how I know that?" Uncle Jimmy said, pleading. "I thought he come back with you."

"He *ran* from me," Marva said. "I turned my switch on him; I whipped his hands. I slapped his face, too. I would've done more, I was so mad, but my Willie Bea has better sense than I do, sometimes."

"You have no right to whup him," Uncle Jimmy said peevishly.

"I didn't whup him. *You* are gonna *whup* him. Get up from there, Jimmy. You find Big and give him what he's got comin'."

"Marva, it Sunday . . ." They couldn't hear what else Uncle Jimmy had to say. Willie Bea had felt she could almost hear Gramp and Uncle Donald being quiet in the front room. Goodness. She would have hated to be in there. She knew darn well that if she'd been her mama, she wouldn't've had the heart to go after Uncle Jimmy. How could you go after someone who would melt away from you, just like hot vanilla ice-cream?

Anyway, that's the way it happened, Willie Bea finished thinking. She hugged her knees, sitting on Gramp's cement steps.

Uncle Jimmy hadn't bothered to move his car. He had cut across his field over to his house. Willie Bea didn't know whether he had found Big and Hewitt and Little. If he had—and he probably had: he knew all of their hiding places by now—it would be Big who would get it.

Poor Big! Let it not hurt him too much. Oh, let Little get it just once!

Willie Bea sat there, rocking back and forth, listening to sounds coming through the screens of the close, Sunday-cooking house. Surveying the whole scene before her. Her own house, which was quiet, although her mama and Bay Brother were inside. After Uncle Jimmy, her mama had gone back home. The Dayton road was quiet. It might stay empty of automobiles for long periods on Sunday. All homes prepared the Sunday meal about this time. Even the farmers who must harvest through the night would break for Sunday supper. Willie Bea let the wonder smells of food cooking surround her and make her mouth water. Once she closed her eyes in order to separate turkey aroma from cranberry, pumpkin pie from candied sweet potatoes. Sitting still like that, breathing the smells, her empty stomach churned.

Haven't had a thing all day but some of Papa's black coffee. My, I forgot to eat my toast and bacon!

It didn't matter now that she'd forgotten her breakfast. For all at once she spied something gleaming, something white, way off down the road. Almost hidden by surrounding trees, she studied that glimpse of white a moment. She cupped her hands around her eyes to see better.

"Yes. Yes!" she whispered and leaped from the porch. Willie Bea was across the road in a flash. She needn't look down the road now. But she did, couldn't help herself. And then she saw that rolling gait, that man, white shirt and dark blue pants; shirt sleeves rolled up above his elbows. Carrying his suit jacket, and the weather had turned cool. Still, he would not roll his sleeves down. When she saw the light of her life in the gleaming, starched white shirt, she sped inside her house.

She wouldn't tell her mama, not yet. Willie Bea heard her mama in the kitchen. Very quietly, she closed the screen and turned right, where the stairs began behind the front door. She took the stairs two at a time, making no sound in her bare feet. She knew where to walk on the stairs so as not to cause them to creak.

She went into the west bedroom, which she shared with Bay and Bay Sis. There was her brother asleep in his crib. The crib had three slatted wood sides. The fourth side was pushed up against the wall. And it was missing its wood slats. Bay could get out of the crib any time he wanted simply by planting his feet against the wall and pushing. The crib would roll away every time, and Bay would climb out.

Now, Willie Bea saw that her brother was asleep. But he was fretful in his sleep, making slight moaning sounds.

He'll wake up any minute, Willie Bea thought.

She knelt down beside the double bed she shared with her sister and felt underneath. Found four shoes and chose the larger pair that were her own.

She pulled out the Mary Janes that had her stockings bunched inside. The shoes were black patent leather with just one strap across the instep. Her sister had shoes exactly like her own, only smaller. They were the best shoes Willie Bea and her sister owned. They were allowed to wear them on Sundays and when company came. But they wore them only at dinnertime, or to church. They never wore them while running around in the grass or in the fields. Bare feet were fine for that type of play.

Hurriedly, Willie Bea pulled on her brown stockings, smoothing them up to her knees, and slipped on her shoes.

Rushed from the house as quietly as she had come inside. Down the road she looked, and hurried toward the figure making its certain way toward her. The man was still too far away for her to see his face clearly. But she didn't have to see his face to know who he was.

Papa!

How could she not recognize that walk and the way he carried his jacket just so over one arm?

Mr. Jason Mills, my papa!

Her papa had one bandy leg. It was his right leg. While the figure of him was straight and tall, that one bandy leg was bowed out from the high thigh every time he took a step. It was his only flaw. Not really a flaw. It was the reason Willie Bea could recognize him. And his white shirt. The shirt moved beside the low, mostly bare branches a certain way, in the rhythm of the bandy leg. It seemed to roll a bit from side to side.

She saw now that the arm that carried the jacket also carried the Sunday paper pressed against her papa's chest. In the other hand, her papa swung a large berry bucket.

Ohhhh! thought Willie Bea, for she knew what must be in the bucket.

What kind? Jason Mills must've stopped downtown. The grocery would be closed. But he would knock on the grocer's side door, as folks did every Sunday and ask, "Newby, what'd you have left?"

And Newby Bishop, the grocer, might say, "I got a little chocolate. I got some strawberry. But all the vanilla is gone, Jason."

"That's all right," her papa would tell Newby. "The kids don't care. Just give me what you got."

But they did care. They would take what was given, but they cared a lot about the kinds of ice-cream their papa brought home for a special Sunday supper. Bay loved vanilla. Bay Sis loved chocolate. Willie Bea and her mama were partial to strawberry.

She hurried along the side of the road toward her papa. Waving the whole time.

Why won't he wave back to me? she wondered. And knew why. Well, he might rumple his suit jacket over his arm. And he's got that berry bucket in the other hand.

She kept waving and skipping. When he was no more then twenty feet from her, Willie Bea stopped.

Oh, he was the nicest-looking man! Her papa. His hair had grown silver all along the edges of his temples. He had dark brown hair that wasn't too short, and it was gray, a just-right gray along the sides. He had a big, pleasant face and it smiled often. He had laugh lines around his eyes. He tried never to look worried around his children. Jason Mills worked seven days a week making fancy desserts for a restaurant nine miles away. He was happy to have work in these times. Her mama called what her papa made at the restaurant fancy *deserts* just for a laugh. Her papa hitched rides to work and from work every day. Hardly a day passed that he didn't get a ride soon from motor cars and trucks going and coming on the main roadway on the other side of town. Each day he got up at six and was home by three or three-thirty, having made all of the *deserts* that were needed.

The desserts he made were not like what came out of Grand Wing's kitchen or even Willie Bea's own kitchen. Her papa made cakes with icing and curlicues like nothing

Willie Bea had ever seen before. Grand said you had to have *equipment* to bake fancy like her papa. And only the best restaurants had such equipment.

Uncle Jimmy thought it was a side-splitter that a grown man spent his time baking, and double-boiling chocolate sauce. He and Little often laughed about it. Uncle Donald never said much about what his sister's husband did besides farming and keeping hogs. But when the subject came up, he and Gramp, too, kind of played with their watch bobs.

They believe it's sissy work, Willie Bea thought now. But I know better.

Then her father was there, bending over her, surrounding her with his kind self. Oh, the scent of him! Willie Bea got a whiff of what she suspected was his Burma Shave. She closed her eyes and his face brushed her face.

"Willie Beatrime," he said softly. "I don't know what I'd do if you didn't come to meet me every Sunday."

"Yeah, Papa?" she said. "Really?" She was so pleased to be needed.

"Some Sundays I'm so fed up with walking, I don't think I'm goin' to make it. But then, what I see standin' so still way down the road?"

"Me!" she exclaimed.

"And no other better than you," her papa said.

She took his suit jacket and the newspaper. That way, her papa could put his arm around her shoulder. He did this, patting her a moment. She walked with him, closely with him. And his arm around her was heavy, somewhat, but it was good.

"Mostly everybody's over home," she told her papa.

"Grand and Aunt Mattie Belle and Aunt Lu and Mama, cookin' up a storm."

"A thunderstorm?" he said, acting shocked.

Willie Bea laughed. "Papa, you know what I mean!"

"A *hail* storm, this time of year?"

"Papa, stop it now." She giggled up at him. "I mean, they are cookin' real good food, too."

"I bet they are, too," he said. "And Gramp and Uncle Donald and Jimmy in the front room—highballs and papers."

"How'd you know that, Papa?" she asked.

"If they not harvestin', they have to be sittin' in the front room."

When he looked down at his daughter again, she looked serious. "What else?" he asked.

"Aunt Leah is here," she told. "And guess what? Aunt Leah figured my vibrations."

"Your what?" said her papa.

"My vibration numbers," Willie Bea said. "My vital number is three and my lucky number combination is one-two-three."

"That and a penny will get you a sweet," said her papa. He smiled on Willie Bea. "What else?" he said again.

"Bay Sis got Aunt Leah first," Willie Bea said peevishly. "Sittin' on Aunt Leah's lap. All made up and with a diamond necklace and diamond earrings. Shoot, I don't care."

"You all do make over Leah so!" her papa said, shaking his head. "You just wait till Christmas. Then it will all even out."

"Really?" said Willie Bea. "Oh, I can't wait!" But she

would have to wait. And she did feel better knowing that by Christmas she would have diamonds, too.

"What else?" asked her papa.

"Well," she said. "Big. He did it again."

Her papa was silent. She looked up at him and he was staring grimly down the road. "Papa, Big would never hurt Bay Brother," she said.

"Don't ever say never," he said absently.

"But he wouldn't," she said. "Big wouldn't hurt a soul."

"Oh, not intentionally, I don't mean that," he said. "I mean, by accident. There's only one thing to do, because Big and the rest of you are so sure—too sure."

"I'm not lyin'," Willie Bea said. "Big can't miss. He never has."

"He *can* miss. You must understand that. He can," her papa said. "Anyone can. Just like you and Little can fall from Uncle Jimmy's high beam."

Willie Bea was so shocked, she couldn't move. Her papa knew!

Gently, her papa urged her forward with a slight pressure of his hand on her shoulder.

"You think I don't know what my girl is doing? You think I wasn't a young'un once myself?" he said. "I would be some kind of father if I didn't worry over you and your sister and brother. If I didn't foresee all of the danger there can be for you out in this countryside."

Willie Bea hung her head.

"There's danger enough in this ole world without you makin' some more," he said gently. "Willie Bea."

"Yessir."

"Before your mama finds out."

"What?" she whispered.

"No more. You're not to walk that high beam ever again. If you were to fall, you could be killed. And you *can* fall. Don't ever think you can't."

"I never have," Willie Bea said softly.

Her papa sighed, patting her.

"Well, think on this, then. You know how smaller ones will follow their older brothers and sisters—what if Bay Sis decided to follow you and Little? One time she tries it by herself. What then?"

Willie Bea was silent. She hadn't thought of that. Of course her sister might follow. Even Bay Brother was known to follow after Willie Bea.

After a moment Willie Bea nodded. She did understand. But giving up the high beam was hard to do.

"I want a promise," her papa said.

They were close to home now. Just a corner more and walking to the house was all the farther they had to go.

Why couldn't home be that much closer? she wondered. Then maybe I wouldn't have to say.

She could feel her papa's gaze on her. She imagined the gaze made her head and neck, her back grow hot. His hand on her shoulder grew heavier.

When she looked at him, his face was stern, closed. It was as if a large, empty space had come between them.

She looked away. "I promise," she said. And her heart was heavy. For how could she keep from walking the high beam? It was always there, waiting for her.

"Take this bucket over home," he told her. "You lookin' nice today, Willie Bea," he added, releasing her.

"Thank you," she said. She felt heavy and dull inside. She gave her papa his jacket and paper.

Her mama came out of the house to greet her husband. She came near the road, standing on the path that led to the house.

"Miz Marva," her papa said.

"Jason," her mama said.

"Had a good day," he said, folding her mama close.

Willie Bea hurried over home to have Grand put the melting ice-cream on ice in the icebox. Willie Bea's family had a refrigerator that ran on electricity. But Grand would have nothing but her icebox. And it was true, there was no better treat than a chunk of ice. Wrap it in a piece of newspaper and hold it in your hand. And you, slurping the melt on a hot day.

The berry bucket full of ice-cream was covered with wax paper and had a metal lid over that. It was still cold on the sides. Willie Bea got it over home before all the ice-cream melted.

We'll be eatin' in just a while, now that Papa's home.

Good *desert*, she thought. Nothing fancy. She put the pledge she had made her papa out of her mind.

**5** There were ten at the big table in the dining room. Bay Brother got to eat with the grown folks. He sat in a high chair next to Marva, his mama.

"Kingsley, baby, you want some sweet yams? Look how he growin' on my candied yams!" Grand Wing was saying.

Willie Bea could hear the talk from the dining room when she paid attention. It was as if she were eating in there with all the grown folks. But most of the time she liked being in the kitchen at the round table. In the kitchen, the food was close at hand. There were still green beans in one pot and baked corn in a glass oven-dish. Any time Willie Bea needed another helping of anything, she would scoot back her chair and take a step or two. Get whatever she wanted. Take a hot roll right out of the oven, too. And churned butter from a crock in the icebox. Everything right at hand.

She had grown up eating in Grand's warm kitchen at the table in the corner on special Sundays. From the time she was almost as small as Bay Brother on up. Eating with Big and Little, Hewitt; and then Bay Sister had come along to sit at the table, the last until Bay Brother was a little older.

Being kids, growing, quiet and hungry, enjoying themselves in the kitchen. It was a way of life. So it had seemed.

But this Sunday, Willie Bea would have been happy to eat in the dining room. She would just as soon not have to even look at two of her three cousins. Little and Hewitt. She wasn't exactly enjoying the good food. She stared as hard as she could at Little and half-wit Hewitt as she chewed. She glanced at Big with concern.

Big's face was splotchy red and pale in places. It got that way when he was upset. When Uncle Jimmy punished him. Big had been punished. Willie Bea knew that by the way he had come in the back door of Grand's house, not greeting anybody. With his head down, hiding his face, his eyes on the floor. Big had eased down in the kitchen chair as though it hurt him to touch his backside to the seat. Willie Bea knew why, too.

Uncle Jimmy had gone after Big. And had taken Big to the woodshed. Uncle Jimmy must've whipped him with his leather strop. The strop was made for putting a fine edge on Uncle Jimmy's straight razor. It was leather-covered wood and was an evil whipping board as well.

Willie Bea had to narrow her eyes a moment to get the picture of what must've happened in the shed out of her mind. It was awful—Big, treated that way. She didn't know who to blame—Uncle Jimmy, her mama? Uncle Jimmy had done the dirty deed, hurting Big. But her mama was the cause of Big getting punished.

Willie Bea stared at Little across the table from her.

"You're the one," she whispered. "Causin' Big to hurt. I know who the Gobble-uns gonna get tonight!"

Little looked up. For a shadow of a moment, she was shocked and afraid Willie Bea really could bring on the Gobble-uns. She believed in them as certainly as she feared the sight of witches flying on their broomsticks.

Willie Bea knew that bad children, evil in the daytime, never thought the night would come. She laughed straight at Little.

Little kicked her hard under the table. The pain shot through Willie Bea's shin. But she managed to swallow the food she'd been chewing. She gave back as good and hard as she had gotten. Her aim under the table was sure.

"Ow!" Little cried, and nearly fell off her chair. Big grabbed her glass of milk, which was about to topple. He pulled her up by the arm and straightened her in her seat.

"She kicked me!" Little tried to holler, but Big had his hand half over her mouth.

"Hush up!" he whispered. "You want Daddy in here with us?"

"I don't . . . care," Little mumbled.

"No, because it's Big that will be havin' to care," said Willie Bea.

"Willie Bea, you stay shut, too," Big said. They looked at one another.

Willie Bea hung her head, then glanced again at Big. They were still friends, she could tell. But Big was hurting, ashamed, saddened that his own daddy and her mama were both put out with him. Big always liked to be on good terms with his closest relatives. He couldn't stand having Marva Mills mad at him. That hurt him more than having his own papa mad at him. He thought Willie Bea's mama was the most pretty, kindest relative he'd ever known. Aunt Leah was the most gorgeous and well-heeled, of course. She was just beyond measure of beauty and riches. But he didn't see her every day. Aunt Leah was like a gift that came by surprise. But he couldn't do enough for his Aunt Marva every time he saw her to make her like him. He saw her at least ten times a day. And now he had done the worst thing he could possibly do. He didn't know how it had happened. He hadn't meant to use Bay Brother as a base for his pumpkin target.

They had all been playing and talking—him and his cousin Hewitt. And Little was there, and Toughy Clay had stopped by a minute. Said he couldn't find Willie Bea. Said he was going to Halloween beg with them. And Little had said no he wasn't, too; he wasn't no kind of relative. Then Toughy had thrown some stones right at Little, yelling, "Bull's-eye, Bull's-eye!"

Little had plopped herself down in the grass, this faraway look in her eyes. Big had batted down each and every thrown stone with his hands as large and leathery as Ernie Lombardi's catcher's mitt. Lumbering Ernie Lombardi of the Cincinnati Reds, who they said could hit a baseball as hard as any man who ever lived. Every time Big looked at his own hands, he thought of his favorite catcher, Lombardi.

Big wouldn't allow anyone to hurt Little or any of his cousins. Not Bay Brother, for certain. He knew lumbering Lombardi would never let a smaller kid get hurt. Never. Big wouldn't dare let Little be hurt, also, for fear of what his daddy would do to him.

Little hadn't been hit by one stone. And Toughy had run off, angry at them. Little had been talking softly. And before Big realized what he was doing, he had snatched Bay Brother. Going all the way over to his house with Bay. And getting his bike, with Bay Brother on the handlebars. And Little and Hewitt on her lady bike. And Little standing and peddling, with Hewitt sitting on the seat, holding on to her dress at the sides. Big still didn't know how it could have happened that they bought a pint of ice-cream downtown. Hewitt had supplied most of the money for the ice-cream, being as how he was visiting and had quite a bit of silver in his new Sunday knickers. Then they had peddled furiously to the edge of Big's daddy's wood. It sure was turning into the worst kind of begging time of Halloween, too, as far as Big could tell.

No, it was not a very good time in the kitchen at the cousins' table.

Best not to cause more trouble, Willie Bea decided. She kept her thoughts away from getting even with Little and Hewitt. But Little wouldn't leave well enough alone.

Little had calmed down, with Big watching her closely in order to nip any outburst in the bud. They had all gone back to eating, if not to enjoying themselves totally. Little seemed to have settled down when, very sweetly, she had to be exactly what she was. Little.

"You should see my Halloween costume, Bay Sis. It is the most fine, priddy Little Red Riding Hood you ever want to see. Umm-hmmm! And has a cape, too, and a red mask, too. You should see it. But don't touch it. Mama don't want any sticky fingers on my costume. We gone over to Xenia for the gala street parade tomorra night. Daddy says they have some cash prizes ought to come out to ninety dollars and ninety cent, too. He says he's sure I can win the best-dressed-child first prize of two whole dollars, too. Are yall gonna go? Bay Sis? What costume you gonna wear?"

Bay Sister slowly lowered her fork. Her eyes filled with huge tears.

"You evil little witch!" hissed Willie Bea. And she slung a spoonful of candied yam right at Little's nose. It was a perfect shot that splattered across Little's cheek. Big had his hand over Little's mouth and most of her face before she could move. It never occurred to him to clean off the yam first.

Willie Bea giggled herself silly as Big's hand spread the candied yam like jam.

Little was snorting potato and had gone rigid with fury. But Big held her in his strong hands, letting her tremble with rage until she had calmed down.

"You know she had no business saying that!" Willie Bea said to Big, finding her outrage again.

"What she say? What Little say?" asked Hewitt. "I didn't hear what she say!"

"Oh, be quiet, Hewitt," Willie Bea said. Half-wit! Willie Bea thought. "Whyn't you go on back to You-know-what-to-Beulah?"

"Gone tell Mama on you, too," Hewitt said.

"Tattle-tale, haul your ashes to Beulah, too," Willie Bea said, but without her usual confidence. She was watching Big and Little.

Big was helping Little wash her face at the sink. He pumped the pump and Little cupped her hands under the spout as the water came out. He was talking softly to his sister. But what Big called low talking was loud enough for anyone in the kitchen to hear. He'd never learned what whispering was.

"Now don't you take on Willie Bea, Little. 'Cause she gonna beat you every time. And then I have to finish it, and how'm I gonna choose between she and you?"

"You better choose me!" Little whispered loudly back. "Tell Daddy and you get some more strop!"

"Just hold her silly mouth under the pump for ten min-ute," Willie Bea called over her shoulder. She went back to eating. But she kept her face to one side so she could move quickly if Little should try to pull her hair or throw corn in it, or something.

No, it was not a good time in the kitchen among the Wing cousins this Sunday of company and Halloween. Little didn't make a move toward Willie Bea. That was because Big kept one of his leather paws on her until she had sat down in her seat again. He held on to her shoulder in case she should think about kicking out under the table. He kept his eye on Willie Bea. They looked at one another. And by their looks Willie Bea agreed not to kick Little, nor to say bad words to her.

Hewitt looked from Big to Little and then to Willie Bea. He shook his head. "Yall sure somethin'. What's to fuss about? Want to know what we doin' in school?"

All of them groaned. "Cousin Hewitt," Willie Bea said, "please don't tell us about all your A's and A pluses. Because it's sickening the way you have to be the teacher's pet because you are afraid to walk home after school. Unless she hold your hand, too."

"That's a lie!" Hewitt said. "There are bad boys all up and down the streets around the school. Miss Hill, my teacher, live only a half a block from our house. She goin' my way, so why not walk her home?"

"Oooh, hooo, he's in *love* with Miss Hill, too," Willie Bea teased.

Laughter came to them from the dining room. The grown folks were busy among themselves. They did not have to fight. But they did fight in other ways, Willie Bea knew. She listened to the good, friendly, family times in the other room. She looked at Hewitt. Poor half-wit. He was about to cry, too. And, suddenly, she knew he *was* in love with his teacher.

Poor Hewitt waited for Willie Bea's attack on him, since she had discovered his weakness. But it never came. Willie Bea felt bad for him and she let it go. He was a cousin, after all, and you did not go after a cousin when he was down. When he had no control over the situation.

That's why Little is so small, Willie Bea thought.

For Little had rubbed it in to Bay Sister and Willie Bea

that they had less than she had. That they could not have pretty Halloween costumes.

When they had finished eating, Willie Bea cleared their plates from the table. It was her job. She was the smartest, not the oldest. No one would expect Big to clear the table with his clumsy hands.

Break all the dishes before he gets them to the sink, she thought now. She did not resent having to clean up after the kids. After scraping the dishes into the can for hog slops, she placed the dishes and silverware in the sink and pumped water over them. The ice-cold water from the well gushed down on the plates.

Willie Bea walked away from the kitchen without a word. The cousins knew what she would do now. And at the kitchen table they waited quietly for her to come back.

Willie Bea went into the dining room. She went over to Grand and stood beside her chair. Grand reached up, put her arm around Willie Bea's waist. The grown folks were deep in conversation. All were listening and taking turns talking. Only a very few times did grown folks in her family talk all at once. When someone died suddenly. Or when there was a scandal in the family. Then everyone might get excited enough to talk all at once. It was quite proper for Willie Bea to come in to her Grand and stand and wait. The fact that she went to Grand, who was the woman of the house, was the right way to do things when you wanted something at over home, her mama had told her.

The grown folks were talking about why Dayton had shut its schools. "Shortage of funds," Uncle Jimmy said.

He would know that! thought Willie Bea. The schools had been closed since Friday.

"Might stay closed for two whole months," Gramp said.

I sure wouldn't like that, Willie Bea thought. Glad I don't live in Dayton, too.

Then they were talking about luck in the form of a $142,800 winning ticket on the Irish Sweepstakes.

"It has tumbled into the laps of Elwood and Ellis Howe," said her father. "They're the managers of a trucking firm down in Cincinnati."

Willie Bea thrilled at how her father knew so much.

"Where you hear about that?" asked Uncle Donald.

"It was in the Xenia paper," said her father. "And on the radio, too."

"Which one is the wife—Ellis?" asked Aunt Lu.

Beautiful Aunt Leah's low laugh swelled out around them. She held Bay Brother on her lap, bouncing him on her knee. Bay Brother wore fresh Sunday clothes and had a shiny silver fifty-cent piece squeezed in his little hand.

Willie Bea's eyes nearly popped out of her head at the sight of the gleaming half-dollar. She never seemed to get the first chance at Aunt Leah any more. Was she growing too big to be the kind of child Aunt Leah loved?"

"They're brothers, Lu," said Marva Mills, talking about the Sweepstakes winners. She shot a warning glance at her sister, Leah, to behave herself.

"Two red-headed brothers," said her father. "Two of seven Americans who'll receive first-prize money in the Irish Sweepstakes."

"Any darker folks win some of that money?" asked Uncle Donald.

"That they didn't say," said her father.

"Probably keepin' it a secret," said Grand, and they all laughed.

Smiling, Grand squeezed Willie Bea to her and looked up to see her, surprised she was there. "What is it, baby?" she asked Willie Bea.

"Grand, we all finish with supper. I cleared the table good. Can I cut us up some pie?"

"Ain't she sweet?" said Grand to everyone. "Willie Bea always take care of the cousins so well!"

"Who she take after?" asked Aunt Leah suddenly. "Commere, baby," she said.

Willie Bea couldn't believe it was happening. She waited as she knew she must. And Grand released her. She walked around the table to Aunt Leah, who sat beside her sister, Marva. And stood there as quietly as she could.

Willie Bea's mama was almost smiling, as if she knew what was going to happen. And wasn't quite sure she approved of it.

"Who you take after, girl?" Aunt Leah said, hugging Willie Bea.

"My mama," said Willie Bea, against Aunt Leah's lovely face. She could smell such powder and perfume, it took her breath!

"See there?" said Aunt Mattie Belle. "She know who she take after."

"No, she don't," said Aunt Leah. "She take after me because she's beautiful."

"Sweet mercy me!" said Marva Mills, and they laughed again at the sisters, who were both fine-looking women.

Aunt Leah gave Willie Bea a kiss on the lips and slipped a new, shiny half-dollar in her hand. Willie Bea slowly raised her hand to look at it. She couldn't believe it. Fifty-cent piece was one costume. And she could buy one tomorrow. But she would have to ask Big if she could go to the gala parade in Uncle Jimmy's car. No. Oh, no! She couldn't go.

"What she frownin' about? What you frownin' about, baby?" Aunt Leah said to Willie Bea. "Hmm, honey, what is it?" For Willie Bea had put on a long face, although she hadn't meant to. She felt like crying. And she would hate to give the fifty-cent piece back, but she might have to.

She looked up from her hand holding the money to Aunt Leah. And had to say it. "Do you have a new half-dollar for my sister, too?" Her voice hardly above a whisper.

"Now that's somethin'," said Grand. "Child got more heart than most grown folks."

"Sure, I got a half-dollar for your sister," said Aunt Leah. "Precious baby, I knew you'd ask, Willie Bea. And here's one for Big and Little and for Hewitt—okay? You give them the money. Be messenger to the fortune lady!" She smiled a winning smile at Willie Bea.

"Lemme see your palm," Aunt Leah said quite suddenly, grabbing Willie Bea's left hand. She ran her index finger along the middle of Willie Bea's palm. Her red-painted fingernail was long and sharp. Bay Brother snuggled against her.

Willie Bea giggled. "Aunt Leah, it tickles!"

"What does it read?" asked Grand.

"Mama, don't encourage Leah," scolded her daughter Marva.

Jason Mills laughed. Everybody was looking interested, though. Gramp leaned forward, proud his daughter Leah was a prophet.

"Oh, this child!" said Aunt Leah. "See that lifeline—it fated, crossed by fate. But the line is long, very long. Oh, it's a fine, strong lifeline."

"What's it mean?" whispered Willie Bea.

"Means a long, good life. Oh. Oh, my goodness, looka this! This child's got the Star of Venus in her palm."

"Where?" Willie Bea's legs felt like they might buckle under her. She studied her palm, but had no idea what a Star of Venus was.

"Right there, on the ground of Apollo," said Aunt Leah, pointing. "There is that five-pointed Star. Venus is a planet, but it's called the evening star, too. And I have never seen such a Star of Venus in *nobody's* palm, it that rare."

"What it is?" asked Gramp.

"Luck," said Aunt Leah softly, tossing her page-boy. Aunt Leah's hair always looked beautiful, was Willie Bea's opinion. "Most fine, impossible good luck," Leah went on. "You will chance to see what the world has to offer, Willie Beatrime. You will know the strange and the unknown. You will win the world!"

"I don't doubt that for a minute," said Willie Bea's papa, grinning at Willie Beatrime.

"Leah, don't you scare her with all that nonsense," said Willie Bea's mama.

"Shhh, it's Halloween!" said Grand, smiling.

"*'A-list'nin' to the witch-tales 'at Annie tells about,'*" murmured Aunt Lu, reciting again.

Willie Bea saw the Star in her hand and thrilled at her great good fortune.

"That's nice we got somebody in the family with *talent*," said Aunt Mattie Belle sweetly. She was talking about Leah and not Willie Bea. "After supper, you read my Hewitt's palm, Leah. He do so well in school. He so filled with the *talent*. I know he's got to be lucky."

Willie Bea didn't care about anything now but what was warm and wonderful inside herself. She skipped from the dining room with fifty-cent pieces clutched in her hands. She felt as light as air.

"Leah, Leah," Willie Bea heard her mama say, still scolding. "You've looked in Willie Bea's palm fifty times, at least, since she was born, and how come you never tell us about a Star before now?"

Willie Bea could hear the grown-ups chuckling. She didn't care at all.

Aunt Leah! Luck! A great Star of . . . Venus! Oh! she thought. There was no better place to be on a Sunday in October 1938 than home with her family. Such luck she had! And all the new fifty-cent pieces to give out. More luck! What else, luck?

*Like to die, pumpkin pie!*

Willie Bea was in the kitchen ready for the good luck of pie.

"Have I got a surprise!" she said to them, still at the table.

"What goin' on in there?" asked Bay Sister.

"Too much!" said Willie Bea. "But looka this!"

"For you, and for you, for you and for you," she said. She gave Little her fifty-cent piece last.

"Oh!" said Bay Sister, her eyes huge and dark. "Money!"

"Not just *money*, it's a half-dollar piece from Aunt Leah. *Magic* money," Willie Bea said. "You know why? 'Cause Aunt Leah's a *fortune* lady, that's why. And guess what?" Willie Bea said.

"What?" asked Big, right on cue.

"Beatrime Mills is the luckiest person in the whole world. Aunt Leah say so. She saw it in my palm."

"She read your palm? Why come she read your palm!" said mean Little.

"She *asked* to read it," said Willie Bea. "She knew there was something famous there. And there was. The Star of Venus is in my palm!"

They looked at her, uncomprehending. The money in hand meant more to them right at the moment than something marking her palm.

"But why come she give us so much money?" asked Big. "And we not even ask for it." He stared at his gleaming fifty-cent piece. "Bet if I'da been there, she'da give us more."

"Un-huh," said Little. "'Cause for his size," she said about her brother. "Aunt Leah'd sure give Big more 'cause his heighth is big as anything."

"You all are stupid," muttered Willie Bea, and changed the subject. "Here. They say for me to dish out the pie. What you all want?"

"I want pumpkin," said Bay Sister.

"Pumpkin, me," said Hewitt.

"Me, too," said Willie Bea.

"Well, not me," Little said. "Give me lemon meringue. Give Big some, too."

"I want pumpkin," said Big.

"No, you don't!" Little told him.

"Little, can't you let him pick his own pie? For goodness sakes," said Willie Bea. And realized she sounded just like her mama. That made her smile.

Little had to say lemon meringue just to make more work for me, thought Willie Bea. But she really didn't mind.

The pies cooled on the counter next to the screen door now. They had first been placed on the round kitchen table. Then they had been moved when the table was set for the cousins.

Willie Bea cut the pies. "Big, what kind you want for yourself?" she called to him.

When he said nothing, Willie Bea knew he couldn't decide.

"I'll give you one piece a pumpkin and one lemon meringue. There's plenty and you *need* each of them," she told him, serving him right after she had served Bay Sister her piece of pumpkin.

"Thanks, Willie Bea," said Big. Big's hands were so big, they seemed to smother the fork he held.

"Whyn't you just pick up a piece of it in your hand?"

asked Willie Bea. So that's what Big would do, once everyone was served. He looked relieved, and set the fork down. Using his hands to eat pie was easier for him than using a little fork.

"Is there any whip-cream?" asked Bay Sister.

"Wait till I serve everybody," Willie Bea said. "You have to wait."

They all waited for her, quietly and politely.

Like they're my own children, Willie Bea thought, carefully cutting pie. She felt excited. Here she was, the boss of them. She seemed to know how to handle them. Even bad Little, most of the time. She was to take care of them and serve them. Luck again! It made her feel most proud. For a second she thought she felt that Star of Venus just itching in her palm.

Willie Bea served Little, and served herself last. "Now," she said. She brought out her papa's ice-cream and a quart and a half of whip-cream she found surrounded by chunks of ice in the icebox.

"Ohhh! Looka that!" said Hewitt. "I want—"

"I'll give you both, wait a minute," Willie Bea said. She found two large wooden spoons. First she spooned the softened ice-cream next to Hewitt's pie on his plate. Then she spooned whip-cream directly atop the piece. She did the same for her sister and for Little and herself.

They watched her closely to make sure their portions were the same size. Willie Bea smiled at that.

"I don't want any," Big told her. His eyes looked like they would eat the ice-cream and whip-cream.

"I'll give you a bowl," Willie Bea told him. "You can eat

ice-cream with whip-cream on top of it. Use a tablespoon, too."

She fixed Big with a large amount in his bowl. No one minded that he got more, for he was so large. Then Willie Bea put the ice-cream and whip-cream away and sat down. They all ate. The dessert was so good and they moaned about how good it all was.

Pretty soon, Aunt Mattie Belle and Grand came in to fix pie for those in the dining room. Ice-cream was served, too, and so was the whip-cream. Everybody felt good. All of them at the kitchen table were peaceful, happy that they were cousins in Grand's kitchen.

That lasted only awhile. Little wanted more lemon meringue, which was all right. Willie Bea got it for her. But once she had sat down, Little wanted more whip-cream.

"Whyn't you say so before?" said Willie Bea. She took Little's plate and put a glob of whip-cream on top of the pie. Sat down again.

Again Little wanted something. Ice-cream, this time. It dawned on Willie Bea what Little was up to.

"You've had enough," she said.

"I want ice-cream and you s'pose to serve me," Little said.

"Want your ugly face slapped, girl?" Willie Bea said. Her anger had come swiftly.

"You want this pie in your face?" said Little.

"Children!" said Grand, hearing them. Little and Willie Bea glared at one another.

"Who wants more ice-cream?" Grand said.

Nobody answered.

Why you, Little! Willie Bea thought. She was madder than a hornet.

"No more fussing," Grand said, and put the ice-cream away.

There was a lull in which anger smoldered at the table. In which Big didn't know whose side to be on. Hewitt felt out of place with these children who were so quick to fight. Bay Sister wanted to be in the dining room with her mama. When she had finished, she said, "Be excused," and slid from her chair, hurried away.

Willie Bea pushed her chair back. "I got to hurry," she said. "Get myself and the kids ready for the trick-or-treating."

Big and Hewitt looked startled, for begging had slipped their minds. Still, they all had plenty of time.

Willie Bea didn't make a move to get up. She was hoping Big would ask her to go with him and Hewitt. Hewitt wouldn't look her in the eye. She knew he didn't want her along, she didn't know why. Probably because her brother and sister would slow them down. Maybe because she was a girl, or because she always was the leader of Big. Of course, Big would have Little tagging along. Little was something else. Around boys, she never wanted to stay a girl. She became what she thought a boy was. Mean, tough, just as evil as she could be. Now, Little looked huffily at Willie Bea. The look told Willie Bea that none of them were going to ask her along.

Willie Bea left the table, acting like she didn't care. She made her way into the dining room, feeling glum. She just knew that either Bay Sister or Bay Brother would be on Aunt Leah's lap. But she was wrong. The kids were in the front room playing on the floor. Willie Bea heard them laughing. All of the grown-ups had pushed their chairs back. Uncle Donald had another highball and looked very sleepy. Even Willie Bea's papa had a highball. Willie Bea glanced at the china closet in the corner. It had glass doors decorated with gold wire filigree. It was full of bottles of spirits, an ornamental vase or two, candelabra, silver bowls, and plates of precious memories. A white plate with a painting of a building on it from the Chicago World's Fair of 1893. Grand and Gramp had gone to there right after they married.

Then, Willie Bea stared at her Aunt Leah.

Aunt Leah was smoking! She held a silver cigarette holder on one side of her red mouth. A cigarette burned at the end of the holder. Willie Bea's mama waved her hand back and forth, frowning, trying to move the smoke away. Her papa had his arm around her mama. He and Leah were talking about something. Willie Bea heard Aunt Leah say she was fixing to go, had to get ready for the evening.

Her papa could have married either one of the Wing sisters. Willie Bea knew the family story by heart. Either lovely Marva or gorgeous Leah. Her papa had met Aunt Leah first, at a church social. He took her to a dance. Then he saw the other sister, a few years older. So he had shifted over, liking Willie Bea's mama best of all.

Aunt Leah's face was rosy. She stared into space right in front of Willie Bea. She smiled vaguely at Willie Bea of luck. And blew amazing smoke rings. They were like round, yawning mouths that lazily swallowed the air.

Willie Bea was bowled over by the perfect, magic circles of them.

Aunt Leah of fortune!

There was a blue haze all around Aunt Leah, framing her.

Star. I have a Star, too, thought Willie Bea, and squeezed her palm shut.

But there was no star quite like that one—Aunt Leah.

So pretty hair. So polished red nails, bracelets, rings. So, oh, so beautiful eyes and mouth! Rich of fortune, Willie Bea thought, wizard rich!

Papa. Aunt Leah— Oh, Papa! For a moment she was miserable.

Why come you had to switch?

**6** "Get away," Willie Bea told her brother and sister.

"Willie Bea, don't be so harsh with them," said her papa. "They've a right to walk with me just as much as you do."

Bay Brother and Bay Sister were always in the way. She gave them a hard, mean look to scare them and they quickly went on to walk with their mama.

Willie Bea walked beside her papa from Grand and Gramp Wing's house to home across the Dayton road. She held her papa's hand tightly in hers. It wasn't late, but the sun was going down. The family suppertime was done. The pies eaten, dishes washed and Grand's kitchen all neat and clean.

Willie Bea needed to talk to her father. She kept her mouth shut until her mama and brother and sister were on their lawn and out of earshot. She had slowed down her papa crossing the road. There was nothing coming down the road. There hadn't been an automobile all afternoon.

She was almost swinging on her papa's fist. "You got something on your mind?" he said to her.

Willie Bea could feel her papa's eyes, but she didn't speak right away. She needed the mood between them to be just so. She leaned her face into his arm. Then he put his arm around her and held her tight. "What is it, Willie Bea?"

Finally she spoke. Very softly, she said, "You could have married Aunt Leah." She didn't let her voice care one way or the other.

Her papa chuckled at that.

"Why didn't you?" Willie Bea asked. She looked longingly in her papa's eyes.

He stared at her hard. Stopped there at the side of the road. "Willie Bea, I don't think you realize what you are saying." When she didn't answer, he went on. "You don't realize . . . No, I couldn't've married Leah."

"But you saw her first," Willie Bea said.

"That's true," he said. "But when I saw your mama, that was it."

Willie Bea couldn't understand that at all. "But wasn't Aunt Leah just like she is now?" asked Willie Bea.

"Just like it," said her papa, and began to move toward the house.

Willie Bea held on to his hand. "But why, then?" she said, in anguish.

86

"You think about it," he told her. He wasn't angry. But he looked hurt at her. She didn't quite understand that look. "You think about your mama, solid and rock steady. Think about who is there for you when you get up in the morning and go to bed at night. I think about that every day," he said, almost in a whisper.

Her papa let her hand go and went into the house. She was right behind him. Something in the way he held his shoulders hunched high kept her from grabbing his hand again.

Was she wrong to ask him about marrying Aunt Leah? It wasn't that she didn't love her mama. She thought her mama was just about perfect.

But Aunt Leah, to read your palm and tell the numbers. Beautiful of fortune.

Just me and her, every day and night, Willie Bea thought.

She hopped up the front steps to the porch, feeling out of sorts. Their porch was open with no roof over it. Someday, her papa had said, they would put a "hood" over the porch and close it in with windows.

That will be the day, Willie Bea thought now, going inside.

There was a letdown when she came home, away from folks, after a whole family day. Things over home were always more exciting than they were at one's own home. Big and Little and Hewitt had gone over to Big's house.

Big never had got any farther into Grand Wing's house than the kitchen. He would have loved to thank Aunt Leah for his half-dollar like the other cousins had. But he let Little thank her for him. For Big didn't dare go in and face Willie Bea's papa.

Big had heard that Willie Bea's papa was going to take away his bow and arrows. Hewitt was the one who'd heard Big's own papa and Willie Bea's papa having words about it. The cousins had been shooed outside so the kitchen could be cleaned up. Only, Hewitt had to run in now and then to speak to his mama. Aunt Mattie Belle and Hewitt were like close friends more than a mother and son.

But Hewitt said he had heard Uncle Jason tell Uncle Jimmy to bring him Big's bow and arrows. Jimmy Wing had told Jason Mills to come and get them. Marva Mills had said, "Please, don't fight." Grand had said, "Boys will be boys."

All this from Hewitt. All of the cousins outside, listening to the details from Cousin Hewitt's mouth. Hewitt did know how to tell things. And he could be counted on to tell only the truth. He had more words than anyone Willie Bea knew, and he certainly could remember to put them together just the way they had been spoken by the relatives.

Hewitt told what Uncle Jason had said. "'I'm not asking anyone's opinion on this subject. This subject is between Jimmy and me. Right is right. That boy with a bow and arrow is a menace. Either you take it away from him, Jimmy, or I will.'"

Then Gramp Wing had said to his very own son Jimmy Wing: "'Jason's right, Jimmy.'"

"'No business, a bow and arra close to houses,'" Uncle Donald had said.

"'But he weren't close to no houses,'" Uncle Jimmy had said. "'Big was out in my wood.'"

"'With my baby,'" said Marva Mills. "'As if my human child was a *bull's-eye!*'"

So Cousin Hewitt told. None of it had done Big any good when he had heard. He'd covered his eyes with his hands, shook his head. "Man, they gone take my bow and arras, shoot."

"I'm sorry, Big," Willie Bea had said. She remembered it all just as clear. She was upstairs now in her house. In the big bedroom. Bay Brother and Bay Sister were there, too. They were not crowding her, not yet. Willie Bea hardly noticed them, she was thinking so hard. She stretched out on the full-size bed she shared with her sister. Her arms were behind her head. She gazed into the ceiling light. It flickered every now and then.

"Sure, you're sorry now. now that you get Big in some trouble!" ugly Little had butted in, blaming Willie Bea.

"Shut up, Little," Big had said. "Ain't nobody to blame but me. I did it. Nobody else."

Then Big was moving, shaking his head. He would hear no more. He had turned. "Got to go," he had said.

"You goin' beggin'?" Willie Bea had asked. Couldn't help herself. She and Big were such close cousins.

Before Big could answer her, Little had distracted him. "Bet I can beat you home! Run, Cousin Hewitt, let's beat Big home!"

Hewitt needed to prove he was as fast and country as his cousins. Of course, he wasn't. But right then Little had let him get ahead of her just to take him away from Willie Bea.

Willie Bea knew a lot. But she hadn't fully realized how clever Little could be.

There had run Big, lumbering after Little and Hewitt. He would beat both of them. Willie Bea hadn't stayed around to watch the performance composed and conducted by Little Wing. That's what they said when they announced the symphony music on the radio that her mama sometimes listened to. Composed and conducted. Willie Bea had gone back inside the house to be with her papa.

She knew that Little could beat Big any time she wanted to. But Little never did. And Little never let Big know she could beat him.

But I know she can, Willie Bea thought. Bow legs churnin'. She is as fast as me. She is little, but she can run longer than I can. She is faster than me when it's a long run. I tire at the end of a long run, and she never does.

Willie Bea remembered what else Hewitt said had happened inside the house. After Marva Mills had said about using her human child as a bull's-eye. Gramp had said the final word.

"We know Big don't mean harm," Gramp had said, "but there's a great danger in allowing him that bow and arra." Gramp had looked sternly, with finality, at Uncle Jimmy.

Jimmy Wing had been silent. At last, he'd said, "I'll take care of it."

He and Aunt Lu had prepared to leave. But they had stayed awhile, chatting with Aunt Mattie Belle and Uncle Donald. All had tried to smooth over ruffled feelings.

That was when Willie Bea's family also prepared to leave.

Marva and Mattie Belle and Lu had done the dishes with Grand, cleaned up the kitchen. It was so nice in that good, warm kitchen again. No one would have guessed such a big dinner had been cooked in there, except for one pie left. One apple pie, left on the counter. It gave away the fact that a big Sunday dinner had been made this day. Everybody but Aunt Leah took some of Aunt Lu's turkey home.

The men had moved off into the living room, turned on the radio again. Aunt Leah was left by herself at the dining-room table. Willie Bea sat with her. And although Aunt Leah smiled at her from time to time, she didn't seem to want to talk. She looked lonesome, smoking one cigarette after another. Then Willie Bea and her family had said their goodbyes.

Her mama gave Leah a peck on the cheek. "See you," she had said.

"See you soon, sister," had come the girlish reply from Aunt Leah.

Her papa gave Aunt Leah a brotherly kiss on the cheek. "See you, Leah," he had said.

She had smiled at him. Her lips formed "Bye," but she didn't say it. Willie Bea could tell that she had her mind on things other than her family.

Aunt Leah had looked all around the room and then said, to no one in particular, "There's something about this day." She rubbed her hands up and down her arms. "There will be a chill on the night, I can feel it already."

Then she had quickly gathered her things together and left the house in a flurry of hugs and giddy kissing of Grand and Gramp. She was gone. They heard her car going swiftly away.

By way of saying goodbye, uncle Jimmy and her papa had nodded at one another. That was all. Aunt Lu and her mama had smiled and pretended nothing was wrong between them. There wasn't really, not between *them*. They were both mothers, both loved their children beyond words. In silence, they understood one another.

Willie Bea lay stretched out on the bed, thinking so hard about what had transpired over home. She was right in the middle of the big bed so neither Bay Brother nor Bay Sister could come hog it from her. Her brother and sister ran in and out, chasing one another. They pretended not to notice Willie Bea, but she knew they were growing more impatient and excited. It was getting late. But still she lay quite still with her eyes closed, to show Bay Sister and Bay Brother that patience was the best. And that good things came to those who waited.

Nothing to do downstairs, Willie Bea knew. Her papa would be reading the Sunday papers. Her mama would be sitting there with him, listening to the radio. They called being together like that in the living room their Sunday time. Was that all there was to do when you were grown—just sit and read, sit and listen? If it was, Willie Bea knew she never wanted to grow up.

Bet Aunt Leah's not sitting down somewhere. No, sir, not her, she thought. She imagined Aunt Leah getting dressed for a Halloween ball. Oh, Aunt Leah would look beautiful in a long dress like Cinderella's! And a gent in a tuxedo!

She wished that this one time Aunt Leah had taken her home.

Oh, take me home with you forever. Then I won't care about begging or making costumes for brats!

Willie Bea made an ugly face and turned over on her stomach. Hid her head under the pillow. She knew that, all over town, children were thinking about getting ready for the Halloween begging time. She supposed all the children in the whole state and country were doing just about the same thing. Kind of slowly preparing themselves for a long, scary night outside. Going up to people's doors. Knocking. Yelling, "Trick or treat! Trick or treat!" And if a person at a door shook his head and closed the door, or if he would not come to the door and you knew there was someone home, well, then you smashed their pumpkins, or spread ugly faces on their windows with lye soap. Goodness! Begging was the most fun of anything. And if folks were really witch mean and haunted-ghost mean and you knew they would never give a child anything, then you got a bunch of chaps and threw great logs on their wood verandas. And, oh, what a roar a falling log could make, hitting a porch! You would run for your lives into the dark, dark night. And try to find one another in the pitch black. And grab a tree trunk by mistake. With dread, hear that tree trunk seem to breathe. And scream your head off as a chap jumped back in shock and fear and ran out from behind the tree.

Usually, folks preferred to give treats. Willie Bea always

93

came home with a sack full of popcorn and apples. So did Bay Sister. Maybe an orange. Would they get enough this year, with Bay Brother going out treating with them for the first time? Hard-tack candy, homemade. Once in a while Willie Bea would discover some of the best chocolates with cream centers at the bottom of her sack. And not remember who had given them. How could she be sure to return to that house next Halloween?

And candy corn. They got lots and lots of that, out begging. Oh, it was the grandest old time!

What did I do with the money! Willie Bea held on to her pillow. For a moment she had thought she'd lost the money Aunt Leah had given to her. But now she remembered she had placed her half-dollar in her bureau drawer. She'd put her brother's and her sister's half-dollars in their bureau drawers.

She could hear the radio downstairs. It sounded like some gangster was emptying his derringer in the uncertain direction of The Shadow. She could hear The Shadow's weird, scary laugh and she knew that, again, he had not been hit. Willie Bea knew, like everybody else, The Shadow would never be hit because the bad men couldn't see him. She also knew by that awful scary yet good laugh that the show was about over. It was almost six o'clock.

I bet if that Shadow gent ever came near here, I'd sure see him, she thought dreamily. I bet he would look just like smoke . . . or a Halloween ghost.

She must have dozed, for the next thing she felt was pressure on either side of her. The pressure was familiar. She was awake and knew she must have dozed, because it had to be the kids climbing on her. She hadn't heard them run into the room and climb onto the bed. They must've been listening to the last half of "The Shadow." Most days Willie Bea wouldn't have missed the show. But this wasn't most days. There was something about this day, just as Aunt Leah had said. Willie Bea was sure of it, too. She could feel the strangeness inside her. Maybe she was a prophet, too, like her aunt. As if she were waiting for something.

To happen? To do? she wondered.

Why else would she have gone up to her room rather than be together with her folks, quiet in the living room? And by just listening, let The Shadow come inside her house and grip her deep in herself.

Wide awake, Willie Bea pretended to be asleep. The kids wouldn't stand for that.

"Willie Bea," whispered Bay Sister, not wanting to wake Willie Bea all of a sudden.

"Yeah?" Willie Bea said, loud.

Bay Sister jerked in surprise. "You *scared* me!" she said.

"Heh, heh, heh," went Willie Bea, "*Who knows what evil lurks in the hearts of men?*'"

"Ohhh!" squealed Bay Brother, and scrunched down into a tight ball.

"*The Shadow knows!*' Heh, heh, heh, *heh!*"

"Willie Bea, you do that soooo good," said Bay Sister. "It sounds just like The Shadow."

"Do Jack 'strong," said Bay Brother through his fingers. He was still scrunched down. He loved for Willie Bea to mimic the radio, but not the scary shows.

"You mean, Jack *Arm*strong, Bay," Willie Bea told him.

"Do it," said Bay Sister.

So she did. Oh, she wasn't as good as the chorus that always sang the "Jack Armstrong, the All-American Boy" theme song. But she knew a good part of it solo and a cappella. And she sang it perfectly, and in tune:

*"Have you tried Wheaties?*
*They're whole wheat with all of the bran.*
*Won't you try Wheaties?*
*For wheat is the best food of man!*
*They're crispy and crunchy the whole year through.*
*Jack Armstrong never tires of them*
*And neither will you.*
*So just buy Wheaties,*
*The best breakfast food in the land!"*

"That was good!" said Bay Sister, clapping. Bay Brother clapped his little hands. And felt it safe to stretch out on his stomach on his side of Willie Bea.

Willie Bea loved Bay Brother's big, round eyes, so sweet and innocent. She took his head and kissed his cheek. Couldn't help herself and giggled when he made a face and wiped off the kiss. Then he made it all right by looking up at her adoringly.

She did as many show themes as she knew for them. She did "Hi-yo, Silver! Away!" And hummed the *de-de-dump de-de-dump, de-de-dump dump dump* music. She couldn't do the "Green Hornet" music, though. That "Flight of the Bumble Bee" was too fast and hard for her. But she mimicked the next-best part. That low-purring, awful-fast roadster that was the Green Hornet's fabulous automobile. And she exaggerated what happened to a bad man at the green whiff of the Green Hornet's gas gun.

Then she did as much of the "Little Orphan Annie" sketch as she could. First came the drone of an airplane, like the "Captain Midnight" sound. Then came a train whistle and the *hoot, hoot* of a steam engine. The "Annie" theme was played on an organ. Willie Bea made as much of the sounds as she could, singing what she could remember of the "Annie" song: *"Who's that little chatterbox, with her little auburn locks—it's orphan Annie."* Willie Bea didn't often listen to "Annie." She much preferred the poem by James Whitcomb Riley. But her mama was known to go about her work, singing, *"Who's that little chatterbox?"* just to entertain Bay Brother when he was underfoot.

For an hour Willie Bea performed for Bay Brother and Bay Sister, just to relax them. It would be good and dark by six-thirty or seven o'clock, EST. That was Eastern Standard Time. Willie Bea would take the kids out at about eight. Bring them back about eight-thirty. And stay out herself until nine-thirty. Soon, now, they would start to get ready.

When Willie Bea had done all she could think of—Baby Snooks talking to her Daddy; the Mad Russian from the Eddie Cantor show; scatterbrained Gracie Allen—she did one her papa could do to perfection. A bandleader named Ben Bernie, called the Old Maestro. Willie Bea didn't know all of Ben Bernie's signing-off song, but she knew it was famous. And not knowing all the words didn't stop her for a minute: *"Au revoir. Pleasant dreams. . . . Until the next time when . . . Possibly you may all tune in again, Keep the*

97

*Old Maestro always . . . in your schemes. Yowsah, yowsah, yowsah . . .*"

She ended with Jack Benny's Rochester and then, stingy with money, Mr. Benny himself. It was a skit Willie Bea hadn't heard on the radio, but she had heard about it. Everyone knew it either firsthand or by word of mouth.

"The robber says," she began, "says, 'Mr. Benny, your money or your life.'

"Dead silence from Mr. Benny.

"'I says,' says the robber, 'your money or your *life!*'

"Still no answer from Jack Benny. He waits a long, long time and says *nothin'*," said Willie Bea.

"Then the robber, he says, 'Well?' like that," said Willie Bea.

"And Jack Benny says, all peevish—" Willie Bea paused a long moment.

"What'd he say!" Bay Sister nearly screamed.

"Yeah!" Bay Brother said.

"'I'm thinkin' it over,' says Jack Benny," Willie Bea said. "'I'm thinkin' it over.'"

Oh, how the kids did laugh at that one!

Then, suddenly, it was time to get the kids dressed. Herself, too. Willie Bea smiled at how well they had passed the time without the kids getting sick to the stomach with excitement. All little chaps got sick when you dressed them up and prepared to take them out in the dark.

Not if you know how to handle them, Willie Bea thought, satisfied with herself.

She got up and went to the hall, where her mama's

cedar chest stood against the wall. On top of all the treasures her mama kept in the chest—ironed sheets, blue, and yellow chenille bedspreads that were wedding presents and still in fine condition, Indian blankets—were some old white sheets that Willie Bea could use for costumes.

She took out two sheets and felt her brother and sister on her heels.

"Don't stand so close," she told them, "it's hot up here." The upstairs was still rather warm from the morning heat. The ceilings were low. Heat got trapped in the attic. In the wintertime, cold got trapped up there and fine snow would seep through the old, worn-out shingles.

Willie Bea thought fleetingly of the coming winter and the awful cold as she studied and folded the sheets this way and that, trying to find the best way to make them into ghost costumes. They weren't double-bed sheets, but sheets for day beds, and so a better fit for her brother and sister.

"Me see," she murmured. But somehow the cold of winter had got in her head. She remembered how stiff and icy the bedsheets would get on the bed in Bay Sister's and her room. Their bedroom was on the west side of the house. All the winter wind and snow came from the westward horizon. Sometimes angling west from the cold, cold north of Canada. You could freeze trying to keep warm.

Oh, so much streams of air coming in under the window frames! Willie Bea remembered. We stuff Bay's socks in the cracks.

And if she left a glass of water standing on the bureau overnight!

She shivered at the thought.

By morning the water would be frozen solid.

Willie Bea shook her head to get the cold out of her mind.

"What's wrong with you?" Bay Sister asked her.

"Yeah, wha's a wrong, Will' Bea?" said Bay Brother.

"Copy cat," she told him, but she was smiling at him. She loved the way he couldn't quite say words properly yet. He couldn't say Little's name right, or any word that started with L. He called Little "Nittle." And if Willie Bea told him to say "I love you," he would say, "I nove you."

"I nove you, I *nove* you," she said, teasing him. She giggled.

"'Top it, Will' Bea," he said.

And Willie Bea giggled some more as she led them into her mother and father's bedroom.

Her folks' bedroom was the smallest of the three bedrooms upstairs. The reason the bedroom facing north was empty, across the hall from Willie Bea's, was that Bay Brother didn't like being there by himself. He'd rather be crowded in Willie Bea and Bay Sister's room, freezing. Bay Sister wouldn't dare sleep alone, either. But Willie Bea suspected that when Bay was older, he would want the room.

Her folks' room had its bed facing the windows, while Willie Bea's was to the side of two small windows. Her mom and dad's bedroom always smelled so nice. A mixture of scents, man and woman. Perfume and shaving soap. There were pretty bottles on the maplewood dresser. Her mama's dresses hung in the closet next to her papa's business clothes. Her papa wore dark pants and white shirts always, for going to the restaurant. One gray suit and one brown suit for funerals, weddings and Christmastime at church. The suits were good, with no mendings. They were very well made, even if Willie Bea had seen her papa wear them for as long as she could remember. All of her papa's farmwork clothes—Penney's overalls, old dark pants ironed until they were shiny, work shirts—hung from hooks on the back of the bedroom door. They were not full of hog smell, like the muddy-work clothes that hung outside in the barn.

"Now be careful," she told Bay and Bay Sis. "Don't touch anything. You know what Mama will say if we mess up things."

"Don't climb on the bed, Bay!" she warned. The bed looked inviting to Bay and he wanted to lay his head between the pillows. But he listened to Willie Bea and backed away from temptation.

"Me see," Willie Bea said. "Maybe first we'll put on the sheets. Mama's safety pins are in the sewing basket." She found the little basket in the top right drawer of the chiffonier. Carefully, she lifted out the lovely basket. The basket was made of thin strips of wood criss-crossed in a weave and painted gold. The lid was shellacked wood on hinges and covered with wine velvet. It was the prettiest box Willie Bea had ever seen. She ran her hand lightly over the velvet. Her mama said not to do that too often, else she'd rub the velvet clean away. The box was her mama's treasure. It had been given to her by Grand, and Grand would never say where she got it.

Why? Willie Bea wondered suddenly, when, before,

she had just accepted the fact that Grand would never say.

And why not? she thought about Grand. And had a queer feeling, a feeling that things were changing.

It's the day, she thought. A strange, funny kind of Aunt Leah day, that's all there is to it.

Willie Bea checked her brother and sister's hands before she let them each run one finger over the velvet.

"It feels like . . ." Bay Sister began, but she could not find words for the velvet.

"Feel *soft*," said Bay Brother.

"You're right about that," Willie Bea told him.

"There. Now that's enough," she told them after a moment. "You chaps will rub the velvet clean away." Said just like her mama would say it. Willie Bea knew that "chaps" meant boys, just as her mama did. But still, they would say chaps. Willie Bea would whenever she thought to.

She searched through the threads and needles and found six safety pins. She pinned them to her dress and put the basket back in its place in the chiffonier.

"Now," she said. After that, there wasn't much talking. She found things she needed from her own room. Old pants, a torn sweater for Bay. Knee stockings for Bay Sister. Another old sweater made from angora yarn that had once been her own which Bay Sister could wear tonight over her dress. The angora sweater had somehow got into the washing tub full of hot water. Now it was half its proper size and was matted, ugly.

"Well, they will have to do," Willie Bea said primly about the old, worn clothes. "Keep them warm all through the begging night."

She left Bay and Bay Sister for five minutes to run

downstairs. She had forgotten to light the pumpkins and only now remembered. She hadn't told them what she was going to do. For she enjoyed lighting the candles without the children waiting, watching her every move. It was hard lighting a candle deep inside a pumpkin. And occasionally Willie Bea was careless.

Wouldn't want chaps see me burn my fingers to a crisp.

It was dark, but not scary Halloween dark yet. She would be busy by the time it was that pitch black out.

Downstairs, her mama seemed absorbed in the Jack Benny radio show. They were well into the show—Jack Benny, the comedian, Mary Livingstone and Rochester.

Her mama looked up as Willie Bea hopped from the staircase to the landing, but said not a word. Her mama was resting on the couch, with a throw pillow behind her neck. She looked tired. Willie Bea's papa had finished his chores and was deep in his newspaper.

Willie Bea went into the kitchen and found the box of matches. Then she went outside on the front porch. She took hold of the pumpkin's stump, and the part of its top that had been carved loose came off like a cap. She lit the candle inside the big pumpkin. Willie Bea and her papa and Bay Sister had scooped out the pulp three days ago. There had been just so many seeds. The pulp from a field pumpkin was stringy, so they threw it away. Then her papa had dried the seeds. They would have lots of pumpkin seeds to eat in the coming winter.

Big old red candle inside the pumpkin, partly used up. There were thick tears of wax that had melted down the candle. The tears weren't sad at all, Willie Bea thought.

They made the candle look pretty. And it would probably last through the whole Halloween time.

Willie Bea went back inside and lit the smaller sugar pumpkin on the dining-room table. Her mama had taken the sweet pumpkin to bake a pumpkin pie for Halloween night, tomorrow night, October 31.

The dining room had only one window, on its north side. It was the room that grew dark first, after the sun went down. When she lit the candle, the darkened room took on an agreeable orange-yellow glow. It made bright the dried, pressed and waxed leaves that were like a mat decoration under the pumpkin. Gleaming purple, red and orange leaves. Oh, so autumn nice!

Willie Bea hurried to put back the matches. She placed them high up in the kitchen cupboard where she had found them, out of reach of Bay and Bay Sister. She had to climb up onto the counter and hold on to the round knob of a cupboard door, balancing. She knew all about balancing. She wouldn't bother her papa just to put back some matches.

In the dining room again, leaning close to the Halloween pumpkin. Its blazing mouth grinned at her. Its eyes flickered, winking at her.

As if the pumpkin were saying to her, "Hurry! Hurry up! The Gobble-uns are coming!"

"I know it. I'm hurryin'," under her breath, she told the pumpkin.

She left. And, leaving, she never once dared look too hard into black corners of the Halloween dining room. Cold fear rose up her spine.

Behind her, Gobble-uns could whisper at her, "Got you, Willie Beatrime!" if she so much as glanced around.

7 Willie Bea bounded back up the stairs. The kids were no longer in their parents' bedroom. They had moved back into Willie Bea's and Bay's and Bay Sister's bedroom. Bay had given up trying to sit still. He was bouncing on the bed. Old bedsprings squeaked and groaned. His effort caused Bay Sister to bounce as well. She didn't seem to mind.

"I'm too hot, Willie Bea," said Bay Sister. "I'm about to burn up!" She had put on the angora sweater.

"Yeah," Bay Brother said. "Too hot, I 'bout to burn up!"

"Be still, Bay," Willie Bea told him. "You all been running back and forth. I heard you clear downstairs. And now you are bouncin', messin' up the bed. Stop that!

That's why you're hot. You stay still and calm down, you'll be fine."

Bay Sister gazed steadily at Willie Bea. Bay stopped bouncing. He watched Bay Sister and then began to gaze at Willie Bea also.

"I'm hot," Bay Sis said anxiously. "Can't stand this itchy sweater!" She tore it off.

Willie Bea pointed her finger at Bay, who was about to copy Bay Sister.

"Don't you move a muscle," Willie Bea told him, her teeth clenched. The kids were beginning to get on her nerves. "Don't you say one word!"

Bay stared at Willie Bea, fear rising. He thought to study his fingers.

"Itsy-bitsy spider," he said, pretending to walk his fingers up a water spout. But he didn't know how to make his fingers walk.

"Okay. You be good now," Willie Bea told him. "Me see," she said, and was silent a moment. "Okay. You leave the sweater off for now," she told Bay Sister. "I'll do your faces; then we'll put on everything.

"Hold on, don't move," Willie Bea told them. "You can talk, grin or sing, but don't *move* from that bed."

She ran out of the room. Heard the kids making up words and singing them. Laughing and singing nonsense out of tune.

First Willie Bea picked up the old day-bed sheets from her parents' room. She slung them around her neck. Next she found the white bath powder her mama allowed them to use for their baths in the big tub. They took their baths each Friday in front of the coal stove in the kitchen, in an out-sized washtub. After their baths, her mama allowed them to dust themselves with bath powder.

Smell so good! Willie Bea thought, holding the scented powder under her nose. Suddenly, she felt a sneeze rise. If she didn't hold it in, she would blow powder everywhere.

The sneeze faded away. Willie Bea sighed and went about gathering other items she needed. A lipstick. She took an old, used, bright red lipstick from her mama's dressing table. And a tiny box of black eye make-up.

You put a drop of spit on the black make-up, Willie Bea knew. And then you took a little brush, stirring it in the wet black stuff. And put it on your eyebrows, Willie Bea thought. On your eyelashes, too. Just take a finger, spread the stuff all around your eyes. Make you look like the walking dead! Oooh!

She hurried back to her brother and sister. Bay, his curly head bobbing and weaving.

"You couldn't sit still even if you were frozen solid," she told him, smiling.

Bay's big eyes watched her hands, full of things to make them up. He was still, momentarily, as he thought hard. "Don't freeze me, Will' Bea," he told her.

Willie Bea laughed. "Freeze you in a block of ice." Bay's lower lip began to quiver. "No, no," Willie Bea said, giving him a peck on the cheek. "Just kiddin', little fella. Wouldn't hurt you for anything."

Bay Sister watched Willie Bea's every move.

"Me see," murmured Willie Bea. "I think I'll start with you, Bay Sis. We have to braid your hair."

"No!" Bay Sister said, alarmed. "Aunt Leah fixed it. Don't touch it!"

Bay Sister's hair was still piled atop her head, fixed by Aunt Leah.

"It's a bird's nest now," Willie Bea said. "I can't fit the ghost sheet with it piled like that. And, anyway, it might get caught in a low branch or something. Hurt you, too. And take off those trashy earrings. Those rings, too."

"No!" said Bay Sister. "Leave me be!"

"Then stay home!" said Willie Bea. She turned swiftly to Bay Brother.

"Well. Well . . . ," Bay Sister began. "Okay, I'll take off my earrings and rings." She did, placing them on the bureau. "Braid my hair," she said. "But fix it back tomorrow."

"We'll see," Willie Bea said. "We'll worry about tomorrow when it comes."

It took Willie Bea some time to fix her brother and sister and then herself. She braided her sister's hair in two braids in back and one at the side in front. Next she powdered Bay Sister's face until it was smooth and white. Then she made her sister's lips bright red. And, using the black make-up, she made the space around Bay Sister's eyes and her eyebrows black.

"My goodness," said Willie Bea, feeling a slight chill at the sight of Bay Sister's face. "This is gonna be real good."

"Let me see," said Bay Sister.

"Well, look in the mirror, then," Willie Bea said. They were standing at the foot of the bed now, with the mirror on the wall to one side of them.

"Ooooh!" whispered Bay Sister.

"Now I'll do Bay's face. And after that, you'll have to

put on the sweater, Bay Sis, before I fix your sheet on," Willie Bea said.

"Okay," Bay Sister said, and quietly sat down on the bed.

Bay Brother didn't take any time at all. Just the powder, only a little lipstick because he tended to think it was some kind of sweet candy to be licked off.

"Don't eat it, Bay, hear?" Willie Bea said. "It's just supposed to cover your lips and sit there awhile."

"Why?" he wanted to know.

"Just for the color, bright red," Willie Bea told him.

"Now," she said, "the ghost costume." She still had sheets slung around her neck. She pulled one off. "Bay Sis, put on your sweater."

"Oh, all right," Bay Sister said. She put on her sweater, making faces and grunting with the effort.

"My goodness, you'd think I was making you walk the plank."

"What plank, where's that?" Bay Sister wanted to know.

"Never *mind*, for goodness sake!" Willie Bea said. "Now. Stand up," she told her sister.

Bay Sister obeyed and stood at attention. Willie Bea fitted the folded sheet over the top of Bay Sister's head. She gathered the material under her chin and pinned it with two large pins, one below the other.

"See? Like buttons," she told Bay Sister. "Now. Spread your arms out." Bay Sister did as she was told. The sheet fell away in folds from her outstretched arms. "See, your hands are free and you can keep your sack for trick or treats under the sheet if you want to. Keep your hands warm, too, under there," Willie Bea said.

Bay Sister studied herself in the mirror. "I'm a good ghost," she said softly. "Thanks, Willie Bea."

"Now, Bay, it's your turn."

"No. No. Don't want'n be no ghost!" Bay cried. Big tears filled his eyes.

"Oh, Bay, listen!" Willie Bea said, hugging him to her. "You're not really a *ghost*. What you'll be is dressed up in a ghost *costume*, but that don't make you a *ghost*. You'll still be Bay Brother, Willie Bea's little brother. Who Willie Bea loves, okay? I have to hurry, Bay. I have to get you ready and me ready still."

He studied Willie Bea. "It gon' hurt me?" he asked.

"The sheet—hurt you?" Willie Bea started giggling. She couldn't stop.

"Stop naughin' at me, Will' Bea," Bay said, pouting.

"I'm not *laughin'* at you," she said, trying to control herself. "You are just so funny, Bay. You are a real Halloween treat."

"Don't you try'n eat me!" he said.

Willie Bea collapsed on the floor. "I said you were a treat! Oh. Oh, Bay, you are the funniest. You ought to be on the radio!"

"Jack 'strong," he said.

"Jack *Arm*strong," Bay Sister corrected. She had been quietly watching from the bed. "I'm so hot, Willie Bea," she said, her voice shaking.

"I'm sorry, Bay Sis," Willie Bea said. "Commere, Bay," she told her brother. And she got him ready in a few minutes, pinning his sheet neatly below the neck. "Sit on the bed with Bay Sis while I get myself together," she said.

The two ghosts sat admiring their reflections in the mirror. Dead-white faces. The blackest eyes. Bay would shiver when he forgot he was seeing himself.

"Just like a ghost," he said, more than once. "But *not* a ghost," he would whisper. "No, not. No, not. No-not, no-not, no-not . . ."

"Stop it, Bay," Willie Bea said.

She would be a bindlestiff. A bindlestiff was what her papa called a hobo, a wandering man. *Bindle* was the bundle of belongings carried on a pole by the hobo. And *stiff* was the tramp himself. She put on some old red pajama bottoms belonging to her mama, over wool knee stockings. And a wool shirt that her mama had given her especially for dressing up. In the closet, Willie Bea had a whole pillowcase full of clothes that they pretended with. She put on a wide belt and turned it around backward so it looked like a pirate's sash. She knew that sometimes, when you tried to be a hobo, you turned into a pirate. She didn't mind which way she came out.

She put on a bandanna to cover her hair. And reminded herself that around the back porch somewhere was a broken broom handle. She would tie the bindle to it, so she would look just like the real thing. A pillowcase would make a good bindle. Full of treats, it would look just like the bindles real hoboes carried. While she made up her face, she thought about getting the stick. She could see her way around the porch by the light from the kitchen windows.

But tomorrow she would take the fifty-cent pieces and go downtown. And she would buy Halloween costumes that they could keep for years and years.

Silently, the children watched Willie Bea change her appearance into a man. She had a mustache that curved up at the ends. She had a goatee, a little pointed beard on her chin made from the black make-up. She made red freckles on her cheeks. And a round black mole right over her left eye. Her eyebrows became thick and black. Very carefully, she made her forehead and the sides of her face white with powder.

"There," she said. She put her hands on her hips and leaned back on her heels. Then she strutted past the bed and knitted her brows as tight as she could, looking at her reflection in the mirror.

"Willie Bea, you look *mean*," Bay Sister said.

"Yeah, *mean!*" Bay Brother said.

"Just call me Bad Willie," said Willie Bea. She swaggered out into the hall and back.

"Bad Willie," said Bay Sister. "Oooh! Hi you, Bad Willie?"

"Hi, Bad Wilnie," whispered Bay Brother. Big eyes staring at Bad Willie.

Willie Bea giggled. "I'm still your sister, Bay," she said. "See Willie Bea way behind Bad Willie?" she asked him.

Bay Brother slowly shook his head.

Willie Bea and Bay Sister laughed. "Yes, you do!" Willie Bea told him. "You know it's me."

"Yep," he said uncertainly. And they laughed again.

"Now," Willie Bea said. She looked all around. "Oooh!" she said, staring beyond the bed. She went over and knelt before one of the low windows. Raised its shade higher. "Can't see a thing," Willie Bea said. "Where did all the time go?" All of the windows were black with night.

The children came over and knelt, one on each side of Willie Bea. Willie Bea raised the window a bit. Cool air hit their faces. With the window up, they found they could see some things. Light from the house made it so they could see the shapes of trees. See the dark, wide band of the Dayton road, and lights on at Grand and Gramp Wing's house. Way to the west, they thought they saw the lights from Dayton reflected on the sky.

"Feel the chill in the air?" whispered Willie Bea. "Oooh!" she shivered. Bay Brother scrunched against her. She felt his little hand holding on to the back of her shirt. Oh, it was nice to make a little fella feel safe, she thought.

"Smell it?" Willie Bea said. Her brother and sister nodded, silent. "Smoke," she said. "From bonfires, I bet. Oh, let's get going. Can't be eight o'clock yet. Haven't heard that Don Ameche on 'The Chase and Sanborn Hour.'"

Don Ameche was the smooth-voiced announcer on the radio show.

"*I* did," Bay Sister said. "I heard him on the radio clear back here."

"You did? No, you didn't!" Willie Bea exclaimed.

"Did, too," Bay Sister said. "I heard that Charlie McCarthy's voice."

"Well, if you did, it's good and late," Willie Bea said. "And you can't hear Charlie McCarthy."

"Yes, I did!" hollered Bay Sister.

"You heard Edgar Bergen on the radio," Willie Bea

said. "He's the voice of Charlie McCarthy. He's the ventriloquist that makes the dummy talk."

There were some things Bay Brother couldn't understand and wouldn't try. One was that the wonderful little chap Charlie McCarthy was a dummy made of wood and that the man Edgar Bergen made him talk. No matter how many times Willie Bea had told him, he still couldn't believe Charlie McCarthy wasn't a boy like himself. "Don't talk 'bout it," he said now, holding tight to Willie Bea.

"O-o-kay!" Willie Bea said. She closed the window, lowered the blind and got to her feet. "Let's go, kiddies. We are ready for Halloween!"

"Oooh!" both Bay Sister and Bay Brother said.

Willie Bea led them down the hallway.

"Shhh!" Willie Bea warned, all at once. She stopped still at the head of the stairs. Bay Sister bumped into her and Bay Brother bumped into Bay Sister.

"Ouch! Ouch!" came the whispers from behind Willie Bea.

"Shhhh!" Willie Bea warned again.

There was a commotion downstairs. For a minute Willie Bea couldn't tell what was going on. Everybody was talking at the same time. She could hear her father moving fast from the door to the couch. Then something heavy fell on the couch and pushed the couch up against the wall. Whoever had fallen was quick to get up again because the springs of the couch squeaked the way they would when someone got up from them fast after sitting down on them hard. Willie Bea could tell that was what happened. It sounded like somebody was hurt bad or something, moaning and crying. It was a woman, sounding scared to death.

"What's the matter, what's happened?" they heard Willie Bea's mama say.

"You have an accident with the car?" they heard her papa ask.

"It's awe-fel! It's jus' aw-awe-fel!" they could hear the woman cry, in bitter anguish.

"What?" whispered Willie Bea.

The moaning, crying voice sounded familiar.

"What?" whispered Bay Sister.

"Shhhh!" said Willie Bea. Carefully, she crept farther down the stairs. She had Bay Sister by the hand and she knew Bay Sister would take Bay Brother's hand without her having to tell her. Someone always took Bay's hand on the dark staircase. It was a closed staircase, steep and without a banister. Going down, a person had to touch one of the walls or lean on one for balance. Willie Bea was leaning her shoulder into the wall on her right. They crept down the stairs and stopped again, hidden from sight behind the wall. Willie Bea stood on the final stair before the open landing, listening.

She decided whoever was upset in the living room would feel better once she saw their wonderful costumes.

Two ghosts and one hobo, bad bindlestiff, she thought.

Showing off at Halloween was a custom. Willie Bea always made a grand entrance on begging night. She had done that ever since she was old enough to go out begging. When Bay Sister was old enough, both she and Willie Bea made a grand entrance, with Willie Bea going first. Now all three of them would make a grand entrance, with Bay Brother, little ghost, bringing up the rear.

"It's the end of ev-ree-thing!" the woman cried. "Oh, my lord in heaven, it's awe-fel, it's aw-awe-fel!"

"Aunt Leah!" said Willie Bea.

"Aunt Leah?" said Bay Sister.

"Who? Wil' Bea, i' scare me on these 'tairs," said Bay Brother. Willie Bea glanced behind her to see Bay Brother peeking around Bay Sister's head.

It *was* scary, Willie Bea decided, when you looked up and saw ghosts. A chill ran up her spine at the thought of what it would be like outside when they went begging in the dark of night. And it didn't quite register that Aunt Leah might be in Willie Bea's living room. Willie Bea had spent so much time and effort getting herself and her brother and sister ready. She had been appearing in costume on the landing every Halloween. And it was hard to understand that something might happen that would alter the second grand event of October 30, 1938. The first grand event of the day had been Aunt Leah and her numbers and reading Willie Bea's palm—the Star of Venus! Willie Bea thought suddenly. But that was over, a fantastic ending to the day. At least, in Willie Bea's mind it was over.

Willie Bea eased them down onto the landing. The landing was lighted by the glow from the living-room lamps. She pulled Bay Sister, who pulled Bay Brother, behind her. She wanted the three of them in their costumes to just sort of flow into view. Just to appear there, like Halloween phantoms.

"The Gobble-uns are here!" Willie Bea announced, in as

good a voice as the announcer Don Ameche or that Harry Von Zell announcer. She always said that about the Gobble-uns on Halloween. They stood there, the three of them, as dressed up, as frightening as they could be.

No one heard Willie Bea. No one was listening. For the living room was a crazy, mixed-up scene. Willie Bea froze on the landing, taking it all in with Bay and Bay Sister. The three of them were poised there in silence, unmoving.

Willie Bea drank in what lay before them with wonder at what she saw.

This tall, very good-looking man stood in the middle of the living room. Not her father. The man had on a great coat of dark wool. He'd unbuttoned the coat and flung it open. He had on a dark felt hat that matched the coat. It's crown was dented from front to back, with a stiff brim turned up slightly on the sides. Willie Bea glimpsed a gorgeous tuxedo suit of clothes under the man's coat. Suit jacket with satin lapels. A white dress shirt with gold-like buttons. There was a satin bow tie. The man had on a handsome gold chain draped across his chest. Willie Bea knew there would be a watch in the man's watch fob. The gent's shoes were white, and black on the shiny top front and the sides of the heels.

"Mr. Hollis, do sit down, won't you?" Willie Bea's mama was saying.

But the man, Mr. Hollis, couldn't sit down. For hanging on his shoulder, being held in an almost standing position, was wonderful Aunt Leah of the first event. What in the world is she doing here? wondered Willie Bea.

Aunt Leah had on a full-length, to-the-floor, silky black, honest-to-goodness evening gown. It was the kind of evening dress that daringly bared the neck and the shoulders. It was the first evening gown Willie Bea had ever seen on anybody outside of the ladies in the movies. Aunt Leah had on a necklace of glistening pearls that came down to her waist and were tied in a pearly knot halfway down. She had on gold, low-cut dress shoes with very high heels. She wore a three-quarter-length, Norfolk-type, precious Persian fur coat that must have cost a fortune.

What comes of being a fortune lady, thought Willie Bea, giddy with the richness of it all.

Aunt Leah's hair was piled high on her head, with curls that cascaded down on each side at her temples. There was a black velvet bow ribbon pinned to her hair in the center, just above her forehead. A cluster of pearls decorated her earlobes. Her face was rouged and powdered to perfection. Willie Bea didn't know how any one person could be so perfectly beautiful in so many different ways as was Aunt Leah.

But now Aunt Leah was crying and moaning. Mr. Hollis supported her with one strong arm around her waist, inside that fabulous coat. There were no tears in Aunt Leah's eyes, although Willie Bea could see she was crying. But it was natural that Aunt Leah would dry-sob. It would never do to spoil that perfect, made-up face with real, salty tears.

Mr. Hollis half-carried Aunt Leah across to the radio. He rapidly turned the dial, trying to find something. You could hear garbled voices going in and out of hearing very quickly. Mr. Hollis took his fist and pounded the top of the radio.

"Now, here, don't do that!" said Willie Bea's father. He

looked shocked. "That won't help anything. Tell me what you are looking for."

Mr. Hollis gave a glance around and down at Willie Bea's papa. He was that much taller. Willie Bea could tell he wasn't the kind of gent that took much direction or said quite a lot. There was mostly static on the radio now, after his pounding of it.

"Leah, sit down," Marva Mills said. "Won't you both sit down and tell us what is the matter?" She took her sister by the shoulder. But that made Aunt Leah hold on to Mr. Hollis all the more tightly.

"Oh, my lord above!" cried Aunt Leah.

"Leah, Mr. Hollis," said Willie Bea's papa, "please get hold. Do tell us."

"It's the world," said Mr. Hollis in a thin, tenor voice. "She call me after she heard it, but I already left to come for her."

Willie Bea was disappointed in the sound of Mr. Hollis. A gent his size should have a deep voice, rolling like thunder, she thought. What'd he say about the world?

"What?" Willie Bea's papa was saying. "The world? You mean there is war? It's the Nazis?"

"The world," murmured poor Aunt Leah. She clung to Mr. Hollis, eyes tightly closed. Her silk-stockinged legs seemed weak and trembly. "It's all over," she cried. "Heard it on the radio. The world. *The-world-is-coming-to-an-end!*"

Aunt Leah's legs buckled completely. Mr. Hollis lifted her off her feet and swung her tenderly up in his arms. It was then that Aunt Leah fainted dead away.

Willie Bea saw her sneak a glance up at Mr. Hollis before she went.

No time for anyone to pay Willie Bea and her brother and sister any attention. Neither Willie Bea's mama or her good papa noticed their costumes. All eyes were riveted on Aunt Leah and her handsome gent, Mr. Hollis.

Willie Bea was caught up, too. It was no longer her show. Her grand Halloween event had been snatched away. But she wasn't angry. Like everyone else, she had been taken over. Seized by fabulous glamour.

A prisoner of Aunt Leah's matchless second coming.

**8** There was silence in the living room, and a strong fragrance of roses. Just the sound of the radio, down very low with its static and its whistling. Willie Bea's papa had stopped fiddling with it. Not one station would come in clearly. Maybe it was just the Halloween night and witches messing up radios, Willie Bea thought fleetingly. But her better sense told her it was Mr. Hollis' pounding. Even she knew that something as magical as a radio with what they call its *sound waves* couldn't take that kind of battering. Shake everything up. Her father ran his hand rapidly through his hair a couple of times. Then he gave up on the radio, which he knew to have a weak tube, and turned back to the women on the couch. He stood there, lost in thought, staring at them.

Willie Bea's mama and Aunt Leah were on the couch. Mr. Hollis was sitting on the piano bench, one hand in his overcoat pocket and the other hand holding a lighted cigarette. Beside him on the piano bench was a glass saucer which he used as an ashtray; her papa had got it for him. And next to the saucer was his hat. Willie Bea's papa didn't smoke cigarettes. Of course, her mama didn't, so there were no pretty crystal ashtrays in the house as there were in Aunt Leah's.

"She comin' to now," Mr. Hollis said in his odd, high voice. He glanced from Aunt Leah to Willie Bea's papa. He was talking to Willie Bea's papa, the man of the house. "She'll tell you now. She comin' to."

A moment ago, Willie Bea and Bay and Bay Sister had crept into the room. All three of them squeezed into the overstuffed easy chair facing the couch, surrounded by the heady scent of roses. That was the fragrance of the smelling-salts mixture in the bottle that Willie Bea's mama waved under Aunt Leah's nose.

"Uh-nuh, uh-nuh," moaned Aunt Leah with each pass of the bottle. She came to in stages. Willie Bea watched each stage, her eyes fixed on Aunt Leah's perfectly made-up face.

Bay Sister couldn't keep quiet any longer. She had been thinking very hard. And now she blurted out to Willie Bea. "Where's the end of the world?"

"Hush up!" Willie Bea whispered back. She didn't turn her head around.

"Well, I wanta see it," whispered Bay Sister.

"Shhhh!" warned Willie Bea. "She's comin' to."

"Comin' to," murmured Bay Brother. He was staring

serenely at the couch. He loved the scent of roses. Summer had come to his living room.

The first stage of coming to was an anguished look that contorted Aunt Leah's face. Willie Bea's mama had her arm around her sister. And when she saw Leah's strained expression, she gently massaged her shoulder.

After the look had passed and her features relaxed, Leah's eyebrows knitted together. Her lips parted and her fingers clutched at her evening gown. Willie Bea's mama put down the bottle of smelling salts and clasped one of Leah's hands in hers.

Aunt Leah's eyes fluttered wide open. She didn't look around, she looked straight into Willie Bea's face. She squeezed her sister's hand so hard that Willie Bea's mama winced.

"They've come. They landed," Aunt Leah said, straight at Willie Bea.

"What, Leah?" said Willie Bea's mama.

"Oh, it's awful!" said Aunt Leah, and she began to cry. Now real tears fell and marred the rouge on her cheeks. "Martians!" she said. "From the planet Mars! Landed right there in the state of New Jersey!"

"Now, Leah!" said Willie Bea's mother. She looked alarmed, but very doubtful.

"I'm tellin' you, I heard it on the radio," said Aunt Leah. "It was on the *radio!*"

They were silent at that. All of them. For if it came over the radio, if it was one of those sudden news bulletins, like urgent messages from on high, then it had to be true.

"Leah, are you sure?" said Willie Bea's papa. He stood before the couch, his hands deep in his pants pockets.

"Listen here," Aunt Leah said. She took her hand from her sister's and began to shape the air in front of her as she spoke. "This radio announcer," she began, "starts out sayin' that, incredible as it seems, some strange *beings* has landed in the New Jersey farmlands. And that they are the first of an *invading army* from the planet Mars!" Aunt Leah looked around at all of them.

They were speechless—Willie Bea's mama and her good papa. Staring at Aunt Leah, tongue-tied. It was too much for Leah to be making up, their looks seemed to say.

Willie Bea felt her heart leap into her mouth.

"Now a battle was fought," Aunt Leah continued. "The government sent our army of seven thousand men to fight this *monster machine* full of invaders out of Mars.

"Our army had rifles. They had machine guns!" Aunt Leah cried silently now, and when she could, she spoke again. "One hundred and twenty of our army soldiers survived. One hundred and twenty, *that's all!* And the rest, fallen all over the battlefield, some place called Grover Mill or somethin'. They were crushed and trampled by the monster. Burned to a cinder by the heat ray."

"Heat ray!" said Willie Bea's papa. He looked off then, gazing at the walls, as if some distant light had smacked him between the eyes.

"That just the beginning," Aunt Leah said. She paid no attention to the fact that her face and nose were streaming wet. But Mr. Hollis did. He leaned over and handed Willie Bea's mama his silk handkerchief. Marva took it and gently began dabbing at Leah's face. "It was awful," said

Aunt Leah. "It went on and on. The announcer breaking in on the shows, don't you see? See, the Martians has plowed through the whole state of New Jersey. They goin' in *New York City!*" She paused and took a deep breath.

"Leah, could you be mistaken?" whispered Willie Bea's mama, as though she could hardly breathe.

"She heard it on the *radio*," Mr. Hollis said, and that was finally enough evidence to the truth of what Aunt Leah was telling them. For the bulletin flashes that came over the radio with news of the world were always true.

"And then the radio announcer standin' on the rooftop," said Aunt Leah. "Sayin' he seein' them Martians, tall as skyscrapers. They wade across this Hudson River into New York City. Said now they lift their metal hands!"

Ever so slowly, Aunt Leah's hands rose higher in the air. Willie Bea and Bay and Bay Sister were statues, stunned and tongue-tied.

"This is the end now, he said," said Aunt Leah. She stared at them earnestly. "He said, the announcer said, smoke comes out . . . black smoke, driftin' over the city. People in the streets see it now. Said they are running toward this East River, New York. Running away from it. Thousands of people dropping in the river like rats." Aunt Leah's shoulders shook. "Now the smoke spreadin' faster," Leah whispered. "It reaches the Time Square, New York City. People tryin' to get away, but it's no use! Said they're fallin' like flies. . . ."

As if in a dream, Willie Bea saw Aunt Leah's pearl necklace glisten and shimmer in the light. She was aware she was holding her breath a moment, for fear Aunt Leah would stop talking. Willie Bea had to know everything she could about the Martians.

Not Martians, she was able to think, breathing out, then in, a long, deep breath. No, oh, no. Great Star of Venus!

They would certainly have come from the planet Venus, those aliens, Willie Bea was thinking. And it had been there in her palm all this time! Itching, trying to tell her something.

I'm a prophet, too! Willie Bea thrilled, tingling at the thought.

"The poor announcer," Aunt Leah moaned, holding her head as though it ached. "He one I usually listen to, I think. And he just shut off right then. He went dead on the air. The Martians and their machines just taken over everything. Oh. Oh! Who's to say they haven't already landed here?"

"Now, now," said Willie Bea's mama, patting Aunt Leah. She looked vaguely around at the windows, black with night. Then she noticed Willie Bea and Bay and Bay Sister right there in front of her. Her face lit up as if to say, How nice you all look! She didn't say it. But maybe they had reminded her. "It's a dark night out," she said to Aunt Leah. "It's the night for beggars all over town."

"After that, I didn't listen again," Aunt Leah went on. She didn't seem to have heard Willie Bea's mama. She sat up straight. Got hold of her black evening bag beside her and searched for her lipstick and powder puff. She sniffled and sighed. "I was 'most afraid to touch that radio. But I did. I turned it off, and it about burned my hand, too. But I pulled the plug! I'll *never* plug it in again! Then I called

126

Avery." She nodded toward Mr. Hollis, but she did not turn her streaked face toward him. "That's all," she said. "I just wanted to come here, be with everybody." She smiled wanly. Her chin trembled. "But what I can't understand," she continued, "is how I could've missed it. How I wasn't forewarned *they* were coming."

"You were!" Willie Bea said, at last finding her voice. She gazed at her Aunt Leah. "This afternoon you said there was somethin' about this day. Aunt Leah, you said there would be a chill on the night!"

"Willie Bea, baby!" Aunt Leah exclaimed, taking in their costumes in one swift gaze. "You so right! All dressed up!" she commented, but that was all. "We'd better do somethin'!" she finished, and said no more.

Willie Bea's papa stood there, wondering what to do. "Don't have a telephone," he said absently. "If I did, I could put in a call to Officer Bogen downtown. And he could put in a call to the Xenia sheriff, although I don't know what good that would do." This last spoken to Mr. Hollis.

There was no telephone anywhere around. It was a long, dark mile into town.

"Don't understand clearly what this is all about," Jason Mills added.

Before anyone could say anything or do anything, the front door opened. It swung in ever so slowly, as if the black night had pressed too hard and had pushed it open. Willie Bea's papa jumped back and spun around, facing the door. Mr. Hollis moved back on the piano bench and his elbows hit the piano keys. A great, discordant noise rose from the piano and spread around them. Willie Bea in the chair had her back to the door. She couldn't move. Neither could Bay Sister. But Bay Brother dived down into Willie Bea's lap. He scooted over, his face and head hidden under her arm.

Willie Bea shivered, thoughts paralyzed, as a stream of cold fell over the chair and down her neck.

"Hey, now, don't upset youselves. It just me." Uncle Jimmy's voice. Willie Bea went limp with relief.

She turned around to see Uncle Jimmy standing there, framed in the doorway. He had changed from his blue Sunday suit into his work overalls for doing his evening chores. He'd probably finished them, too. He had taken in their fright.

Uncle Jimmy glanced at the radio, then at his baby sister, Leah, all dressed up and fixing her face, streaked from crying. He noted the tall stranger sitting over there, and the way the gent carefully removed his elbows from the piano keys. The sound of the piano faded as Uncle Jimmy Wing framed in his mind the words he would later say to Aunt Lu: "Leah got herself a new dude." He had taken the scene in in a second, and understood it.

"I heard," he said, nodding at the radio. "Papa say, yall come on over home. Everybody there now but yall." He paused. He did not look directly at Willie Bea's papa or anyone. But Willie Bea felt that he was speaking directly to her papa, listening at him, figuring out how much her papa believed.

Uncle Jimmy cleared his throat importantly. He looked up, gazing at the flowered wallpaper high above the couch. "They seen them thangs lyin' low over by the Kelly farm," he said.

Suddenly, fear in the room was the shape of a poison-snake. Coiled. Rattles shaking.

"They gret big," Uncle Jimmy said, his voice low. "Gleamin' eyes," he said. "V-shaped mouths. Big as trees. Big as houses. Tall as a standpipe, I heard—eighty foot high. Over there at the Kelly farm, on the north of town." With that, he shrugged. Reached behind him. And held up his arm for them to see.

"Got my shotgun!" he exclaimed grimly, looking directly at Willie Bea's papa. There in his hand was his deadly shotgun. He knew Willie Bea's papa didn't own a gun, wouldn't have one in his house. Uncle Jimmy stepped out of the house onto the porch. "Yall come on over home," he said. "There mightn't be much time." He closed the door behind him.

There was something absolutely serious about the sight of Uncle Jimmy's shotgun. It stunned all of them there in the living room. Any doubt they might have had vanished. The snake of fear struck them hard.

"Oh, my lord above!" cried Aunt Leah. Getting to her feet, she spilled powder and lipstick on the floor. Mr. Hollis, halfway out of his seat, folded her in as she wrapped her arms around his neck.

Willie Bea's mama, always neat, bent to retrieve the make-up. Stuck it in Leah's purse. "I'm going over home," her mama said. She rushed out into the kitchen and came back with a modest tin of Halloween candy and her black everyday pocketbook.

"Marva," said Willie Bea's papa.

"You can stay here if you want to," Marva said.

"I didn't say that. Did I say that?" said her papa.

"No, but that's what you might be thinking, to stay," her mama said. She grabbed up Bay Brother, who was quite happy to be folded against her.

"Did I say what I was thinking?" her papa said. "I don't doubt what Leah and Jimmy have heard," he said, uncertainly.

"Willie Bea, come on. Bay Sis," said her mama.

"Can we trick-and-treat now?" Bay Sister asked.

"Trick-and-treat over home," Willie Bea's mama said.

Bay Sister looked about to argue. "Come on!" Willie Bea whispered to her. "Shut and let me take care of it!"

"Huh?" said Bay Sister. Willie Bea's mama was on her way out of the door. She turned back. "Leah? Stop that in front of the children!" Aunt Leah was being comforted tightly by Mr. Hollis. The next moment Mr. Hollis was threading his way around Willie Bea, Bay Sister and their papa, leading Aunt Leah out of the house. They were outside, and Willie Bea and Bay Sister were right behind them.

Willie Bea's papa was left. He might make his way over home. He could walk downtown. It would take him no more than fifteen minutes at the most. Time passed while Jason Mills decided what to do.

He turned up the radio. Stations came in and out. There was static. He didn't hear a thing that sounded like a news flash. And if there had been a catastrophe, wouldn't the news have been on every station on the radio? Just the way the horrible destruction of the *Hindenburg* dirigible had been all over the radio last year?

The *Hindenburg* had been an 800-foot, cigar-shaped super-balloon that was steered and fueled by hydrogen fuel. A radio newsman had been right there a year ago, routinely announcing the return of the *Hindenburg*. It had crossed the ocean from Germany many times before. It carried ninety-seven passengers. And, tragically, it had caught fire as it approached its Lakehurst, New Jersey, mooring.

New Jersey again!

Thirty-five passengers had been killed; and in half a minute the great dirigible was a twisted heap of steaming, molten metal.

Heat. A heat ray, wasn't it, Leah had said?

The Germans, too! They had made the *Hindenburg* and other great dirigibles they called zeppelins. Ingenious Germans!

Hindenburg! The man Von Hindenburg, President of the German Republic, had submitted to Nazi power. He had named Adolf Hitler Chancellor of Germany in 1933. The fascist Hitler!

Jason checked his pocket watch. After nine. The night wore on.

But Germany, the *Hindenburg*, an old catastrophe. New Jersey again and a new catastrophe.

Could it be . . . ? An invasion not from Mars. No indeed, not. But from Germany? Von Hindenburg. Nazis. The fascist power on the move!

Jason Mills turned off the radio, turned out all but one light. He gathered money, keys, a warm sweater, which he put on under his overcoat, and left the house. He didn't think to lock the door until he was down the front steps. He went back up, back into the house. He went into the dining room. No one had thought to blow out the candle in the sweet pumpkin on the dining-room table. He did so. He went into the kitchen and locked the back door. Then he came through the house again.

He went to the closet in the dining room and got Marva's winter coat for her. He remembered she had gone over home without even a sweater over her dress. Next he went to the sideboard and got the life-insurance policy out of his business drawer. No telling what might happen this night. He took his bankbook, too, although there was never much money in his account. Then he went out, locking the front door behind him. There had not been a reason to lock up the house for some time. The family had not been far from home in so long.

He went quickly to the Dayton road and crossed it, going over home. They'd all be talking, over home. Someone—maybe him—would speak about organizing a patrol for this end of town. Or whether they should leave the area. There certainly were enough autos in the family to transport them all. But where would they go? He wouldn't have a gun. Perhaps his axe would do.

Jason Mills strode away in the Gobble-un dark. The huge field pumpkin was left glowing on the front porch. Its pyramid eyes gleamed wickedly. Its light was orange, flickering, gathering in the night.

All over town, in other towns, in cities, the Martians landed. And everywhere, fearing for their lives, the people panicked.

Across the country, jack-o'-lanterns guarded porches. Their gap-toothed grins were scornful. Somewhere, deep a-pumpkin, they laughed in silent, mocking shrieks.

**9** Aunt Leah and Mr. Hollis got to over home first, before Willie Bea and her mama and Bay Brother and Bay Sister arrived. That was because Mr. Hollis had parked his automobile, a long Buick, right in front of Willie Bea's house, pointing west toward over home and Dayton beyond. The automobile was halfway in Willie Bea's yard and half on the roadway. If Mr. Hollis had parked all of it on the roadway, he would have blocked that Dayton road. That was how wide and grand was his automobile.

Willie Bea hoped her papa wouldn't come out and see those automobile tires bound to leave slide marks on the grass, and the auto parked there as if the gent owned the place. But Mr. Hollis quickly got Aunt Leah into the auto in the front seat next to the driver's seat.

Oh, I wish I could ride with them! Willie Bea thought.

She stood right there in the grass, watching, along with her mama holding Bay, and Bay Sister. Mr. Hollis' automobile was so swell—the kind folks called a *boat*, it was that long and sleek. Shining there in the yellow-orange glow of the pumpkin. While the auto door was open as Mr. Hollis got in, Willie Bea could see the sleek inside. Wonderful seats of dark leather. The paneling in front of the wheel and to the right side was deep brown and probably leather, too. Oh, it was a fine Buick, fit for Aunt Leah in her fur and evening gown.

The motor started up and the grand car lunged away, crossing the roadway and pulling up in front of Grand and Gramp Wing's house in a blink of an eye, on the wrong side of the road. And tooling onto the front yard, just like the gent owned that place as well. Then Willie Bea heard the motor stop. She and her mama and the kids had moved out onto the Dayton road now. And they saw two figures fly out of the car and hurry up Grand Wing's wide front steps. Willie Bea could hear Aunt Leah start in talking, explaining away in a fearful voice, before she reached the front door.

Willie Bea and her mama and the kids had watched wonderful Aunt Leah and her gent leave and everything, and not one of them had thought to ask for a ride over home. Well, Willie Bea had thought to ask. And probably Bay Sister had thought to ask. Bay Brother, little ghost, was holding tight to his mama, up in her arms. But neither Willie Bea nor her sister would have dared ask something like that before their mama did. And their mama wouldn't have mentioned a ride just across a roadway and a little-bitty few feet beyond to over home. No point in their even asking her to mention it. They had known she wouldn't.

It was a chill night, all right. An uncomfortably cool, beggars, trick-or-treat night.

"It's airish out," Willie Bea's mama said, starting across the road to over home. "Nobody goes out of Grand's house tonight."

"Are we all gonna die?" asked Bay Sister ghost, all dressed up, skipping to keep up with Willie Bea and her mama.

"No, nobody's going to die!" Willie Bea's mama said. Her voice didn't sound the way it should. It sounded shaky, like it might jump up high any minute.

Marva lifted her face to the sky. Willie Bea did the same. Up there was a wide, deep universe. It looked distant, up there. It looked dark, even though there were lots of stars. And smoky, way up there, too. Like something *could* be wrong with the black night of their world, Willie Bea thought. It was a cloudless, moonless night.

Willie Bea realized she would have to find a way out of Grand Wing's house this night.

"We can go as far as Aunt Lu's house," she told her mama. She was testing to see if she could get away with pretending to go over to Aunt Lu's. Of course, she wouldn't go there, but she would say she was going, if she had to. "Aunt Lu's going to have lots of treats for us. I reminded her about begging, earlier," Willie Bea finished.

Her mama was silent a moment before she said, "Grand

will probably have all such for you all. Don't fret, sister. There will be plenty."

Well, she didn't say we *couldn't* go over to Aunt Lu's, Willie Bea thought, relieved.

"But we're all dressed up!" cried Bay Sister. "We have to go out begging tonight."

"You'll show off for the folks over home!" their mama said impatiently. "We'll have a costume show. Maybe a prize for who has the best costume."

Their mama was making up something for them to do over home as she went along, Willie Bea could tell.

"Little will win it," Bay Sister said about the costume show. "She has a store-bought Little Red Riding Hood outfit. I'm not gonna be in it."

"I'll be the judge," their mama said, calmly this time. "There will be more than one winner."

That was that. There wasn't to be any outside trick-or-treating. And after all of the work Willie Bea had done, putting together their costumes. Well, she really didn't care now. She had her way out of the house, to pretend she was going over to Aunt Lu's. She was just sorry for the kids, was all. Well, Bay Brother was too young to know the difference between begging outside and being treated at home. But Bay Sister would hate to miss the out-of-doors, the scary nighttime without a mama or a papa to keep watch.

Willie Bea had her mind on something else. The Kelly farm was the something else and the reason she had to get out of over home. What Uncle Jimmy had said about the Martians.

Martians! Not them, but *them*, from the planet Venus.

Tall as trees! *V*-shaped mouths! That *V* was the clue to knowing who was *Venus them*. If she could just see them, talk to them and explain about her own Star of Venus . . .

From there, her thoughts were vague and unclear about what she could explain to *them* about her Star. But Willie Bea knew she must be gifted, fated. She knew they, the Venus them, wouldn't mean *her* any harm.

Perhaps they were frightened, she thought. That was why they had used the heat ray. More than likely, they were lost and had to land. Ran out of gasoline on their way back home to Venus. That could be it.

Willie Bea knew where the Kelly farm was. Owned by Kellys. The very name filled her with the mystery of such people. Rich landholders. She reckoned she had seen the sons, older and farmers themselves. They brought their harvested grain through town in wagons pulled by tractors. She certainly had heard of them.

She knew the general location of the Kelly farm, that is. She had never been in that direction away from home. It wasn't that it was so far away. There were some big farms close in to the town. You could see the fields of them just by looking, practically surrounding the town. But the Kelly farm was supposed to be different. It didn't have a farmhouse, it had a mansion. And white columns as high as a hayloft, some said. A place so huge a giant could live there.

Willie Bea was twelve and knew her way downtown and her end of town well. But rarely did she venture to the far side of town, or beyond the town. Girls her age just didn't wander over there. And it was hard getting around if you had no automobile in the family and no bicycle.

Someday she would have a bicycle, her papa said so. If she had everything all at once now, what would there be left to have when she was older? her Grand had once said. Willie Bea had wondered what was the everything she was supposed to now have.

But she didn't miss not having a bicycle. She was used to trotting distances if she needed to go downtown. And stilting on her poles, traveling for fun. She had never before wanted or needed to go to the Kelly farm. Never even thought about going there. They said there was a pond there and rich folks ice-skated on the pond, below this great big Kelly place on the hill. Willie Bea didn't own any ice-skates. She never mentioned to her father she might like to try ice-skating, for fear he would feel bad he couldn't afford to buy her ice-skates. There wasn't much her papa could afford to buy. And that made Willie Bea sad sometimes, when she had time to sit and think about it.

Wouldn't it be swell if times were suddenly to get better a lot faster—say that tomorrow they'd all be living swell?

She wanted a beautiful girl's bicycle someday. A beautiful *red* girl's bicycle.

Over home. They came up the same steps that Aunt Leah and Mr. Hollis had walked. But Willie Bea's coming over home with her mama and brother and sister didn't cause any kind of stir. They came in and the din in the front room was something awful. It spilled down the hallway and into the kitchen. Babies were squalling. Young-'uns Bay Brother's age were hollering and shrieking.

Grown folks gave backhands whenever they had a mind or when wild ones needed quieting. And he that got the backhand wailed to beat the band, causing more noise.

Over home, the world hadn't yet thought about coming to an end. It hadn't quite panicked. But over home was disorder and confusion. There was a disturbing air of dread on the one hand and a mood of serious doubt on the other.

Once inside, it was as if Willie Bea forgot there was a mama or a papa. She was somehow all alone in the midst of everyone. She was there, but everything around her seemed distant. Noise, movement, as more and more folks gathered. They all came with something to add about the Martian invasion.

She could feel fear. Some grown folks over home were afraid. It was in the way they looked around over their shoulders at the windows. They kept watching the front door like they expected it to fly open. To reveal a dreaded monster-thing from Mars framed there in the doorway.

Willie Bea lost her mama at once. Then she found Aunt Leah in the midst of the disorder. Leah was posed in her lovely gown on Grand Wing's couch. She must have fallen into a faint again as soon as she entered the front room. She would have had to, Willie Bea decided. A lot of men surrounded Aunt Leah, crowding Mr. Hollis, Willie Bea noted. And some wives kept shoving squalling babies onto their husbands' knees. Some of the folks now over home were not even relatives, although Willie Bea recognized them all. Toughy Clay and his mama, Honey Clay, and her gent, Mr. North, were some of the unrelated folks.

Honey Clay had never married, and bad boys teased Toughy Clay about that.

Willie Bea felt in a daze. The folks around her were hazy, like in a dream. Individuals stood out and for the rest of her days she would remember what so-and-so said all of a sudden there in the front room. She would never forget how there was always a clump of men bent low over the radio console. Turning the dial back and forth, one of them would bob up and down, saying, "Shhh! Shhh! We can't hear!" And it dawning on him that the little kid bawling on his shoulder was causing most of the racket. Another one of them would have his hand cupped around his ear, with the other hand kind of smacking that console, giving it a spanking, as though that would make it pay attention.

There was still another man—oh, it was Uncle Donald! Willie Bea hadn't noticed at first who he was; she didn't see Uncle Donald so often. He was by the group of men at the radio. But he stood separate. He was watching them, chuckling to himself, shaking his head. "Tell you any-thing, tell you *anything*," he was saying. Willie Bea forgot about him, too.

Suddenly, somebody else bobbed up from the radio. "Shhh!" he said, as though Willie Bea had been talking, and crouched down again to listen hard.

Oh, the fear all around was almost a shape that Willie Bea could touch.

Sweet Aunt Lu Wing was sniffling and crying a little, right before Willie Bea's gaze. Her hair was pulled back in a ball, and strands of it had come loose in wisps around her face. She dabbed at her eyes with a lace handkerchief.

140

"Somebody move that stone piece offen the well," she was saying softly to no one in particular. Covering her eyes with the handkerchief. "I've always been ready for Old Maker. I will jump down. Cold well water'll take me fast. That's the best way. Get it over quick, before *they* get here."

Willie Bea couldn't believe what she had heard. Aunt Lu, ready to jump down the well! She followed as Aunt Lu wandered over to where Aunt Leah was fixing her make-up again over on the couch. Aunt Lu stood looking at Leah in her fine gown.

"Oh, Leah. Leah! Come *with* me!" she said, wringing her hands. No one seemed to be listening but Willie Bea.

Right on that, Gramp came in from the hallway. "Donald! Donald!" he called to Willie Bea's Uncle Donald, still standing apart. "Jimmy's outside, patterollin' the house with his shotgun. Fool is gone see a rabbit move and blow a hole in his own foot. Martians, pshaw!" Gramp Wing looked half disgusted and a part uncertain, Willie Bea could tell. "Go get Jimmy," Gramp went on. "Get that gun away from him, Donald."

Uncle Donald didn't hesitate; he hurried out.

Willie Bea heard herself saying, "Somebody better do somethin' about Aunt Lu. Talkin' about jumpin' down the well herself."

Willie Bea's oldest sister was there. Rebecca Esther Mills Knight. "Where?" she said to Willie Bea.

"Huh?" said Willie Bea. It was as if her sister had appeared out of thin air. "Hey, Becky! Where are the twins? Why come yall didn't come to supper?"

"Hey, Willie Bea. Been too busy. Oooh, Willie Bea! You dressed up so nice!" Rebecca said.

"Thank you," said Willie Bea. She looked down at herself. She'd forgotten she was dressed up at all. "You should see Bay and Bay Sis. I dressed them up," she said proudly.

"Where?" asked Rebecca, looking all around.

Then they saw Bay and Bay Sister on the other side of the room. Near the radio. Over there was Rebecca's husband, who was Willie Bea's brother-in-law, Riley Knight. Willie Bea's mama was talking to Riley. He was now the one fiddling with Grand Wing's radio console. He had pressed some men out of his way. He had his twin babies clinging to his neck. They were dressed like cowboys of the Wild West.

"Becky, did you make them the costumes?" Willie Bea asked her sister.

"Uh-huh," Rebecca said. "Took me all last night and this morning."

"They look so cute," Willie Bea said about the twins. The boys had on cowboy hats made of cardboard covered with red fabric. On their belts they had tiny cardboard guns painted black. Their papa had nicknamed the boys Trump and Trick, and that was what everybody called them. "Here, Trump. Hey, Trick," like they were a couple of cute puppies. They were ten times awfully cute.

"But where's Aunt Lu?" asked Rebecca.

"Say she's gonna jump down the well, too," Willie Bea said.

"Mercy!" moaned Rebecca. "Who started all this?"

"Don't you believe it?" Willie Bea whispered, loud enough for her sister to hear.

Wide-eyed, Rebecca looked all around, not at Willie Bea. She shook her head. "Don't know," she said. "I didn't hear anything on the radio. Haven't seen nothin' outside. But the sky tonight does look dark and smoky, some."

Willie Bea smiled and nodded encouragingly.

Then Riley was standing there in front of Willie Bea. The twins were bouncing in his arms. "Can't get nothin' on the radio," he said. "Wouldn't be able to hear nothin' if I could get somethin'.

"Hey, Willie Bea," he said. He had to shout, almost. "You lookin' real like a hobo."

"Hey, Riley," she said. "Lemme hold Trump."

He looked proudly at his boys. "He too heavy for you, Willie Bea. Anyway, you might get him full of paint and powder."

"Oh, that's right," Willie Bea said. She saw her mama over across the room, talking to a man and a woman. And her sister Rebecca, right beside her, was telling Riley about Aunt Lu.

Through the din of voices and the static turned up so loud on the radio, Willie Bea recognized the woman standing next to her mother as Honey Clay and the man as Mr. North. Grand and Gramp Wing's house had turned into a real social gathering.

Willie Bea glanced at the kitchen. She thought she saw Little in there. If there had been a bunch of young'uns in the kitchen, she would have known there were treats in a big bowl in there. But she couldn't hear or see any bunch of older kids, although they had to be around somewhere. Aunt Lu probably hadn't remembered to bring her treats.

Good, Willie Bea thought.

Then she noticed that Aunt Leah was no longer sitting on the couch, glamorous. She was nowhere to be seen.

Oh, Willie Bea thought, what must I do about it? She knew she should do something about the fact that Aunt Leah was nowhere to be seen. But there were too many sights and sounds. She couldn't keep her mind fixed to any one thought.

Mr. Hollis was standing up and another man who had been seated was standing with him. It was Willie Bea's oldest brother, Jason Mills, Jr.

Jason!

A little girl about the age of Bay Brother clung to his hand. She had on a red nightgown and a red, pointed cap that had a bell at the end of it. Every time she looked around, the bell tinkled high and pretty.

Willie Bea didn't get a chance to go over and talk to Jason Jr. and the baby girl, who was Jasonia, named after her father. Willie Bea looked, but she didn't see Jason Jr.'s wife, who was Marcia Fay. She suspected that Marcia Fay must've had some of her own relatives over for dinner this Sunday. Her family was the Ramsey family. That was why Jason Jr. and Marcia Fay and the baby hadn't come for Grand's fine supper.

Right before her eyes, there was Toughy Clay staring, peering at her. Like he was the sudden shape of noise and autumn colors of orange and gold. A slight touch of black. Just all of a sudden, Toughy, right smack in front of her.

"Where'd you come from?" Willie Bea cried.

"I'm just here!" Toughy yelled back, happy as he could be to be somewhere, and a part of noise and action. He was dressed up like an ear of field corn with its pale, dry husk still clinging over the corn. A sheet, dyed orange and gold, wrapped around him and pulled high in a point behind his head. He had drawn on an old shirt to make corn kernels. The corn kernels were sketched down his shirt front, down his shoulders and arms, peeking out of the husk-sheet. His face was powdered a sickly gray, like some larva-borer in the corn.

"You are a picture of an ear!" Willie Bea told him. His was a swell costume.

"I like your hobo, too," he said, and then, "Guess what?"

"What?" she said.

"They landed at the Kelly farm," Toughy said.

"I know that," Willie Bea said. To hear Toughy say it made her cold and still inside. It was all true.

"Well, you don't know this," he said. "I saw one. Gret big Martian man."

"You . . . *what?*" Willie Bea said, barely able to get the words out.

Toughy nodded. Looked away. "It crunched down behind a tree. Hidin', I guess. But it was bigger 'n any old tree. Its fire eyes were in its chest. That's why it thought it was hidin' behind the tree. 'Cause the tree just come up to its chest, where the eyes was."

"What were you *doin'* over there?" Willie Bea managed.

"Just trottin' by," Toughy said vaguely. "On my way

home from town. Just swung over there, see what I could see. I knew they was there long before anyone else."

Willie Bea didn't think to ask why Toughy had gone over there in the first place. "What were they doing?" she said, shivering.

"Nothin', *they*," Toughy said. "I only saw this one Martian, just scrunched down near the Kelly place. Gret big, house-size. Silo-high. Thinkin' about pullin' down them Kelly columns, I expect. I'd had me a gun, I'da taken out one of them flamin' eyes."

"Ohhh!" Willie Bea said, and sat down hard in a straight chair. She hadn't known the chair was there. But she was glad it was. For her legs simply gave way under her.

"Toughy, they're not *Martians*," she said. She was about to reveal the secret that the Martians were actually from Venus. But she didn't get the chance.

Uncle Donald came into the front room in a hurry. "Need some of you right now," he said generally, louder than the radio. He waved his hand toward the kitchen. Grand Wing was cutting chocolate cake and there were tired little young'uns surrounding her.

"What is it?" Mr. North said.

Gramp had come in and was over by the radio now. He gazed at Uncle Donald the ways folks do when they are listening hard to a faraway sound. "If I got somethin', I don't know what it is," he said to Uncle Donald. "Confounded static."

"Well, they got the top piece offen the well," Uncle Donald said. He looked half angry and half fearful. "Jimmy did it. I couldn't stop him. He and Leah wrastle that top stone piece right off with a wedge iron. My li'l sister Leah may be silly, but she is strong to boot."

Gramp stared, transfixed, at Uncle Donald. So did some others at the radio console.

"Lu says she means to jump down the *well*," Uncle Donald explained. "And Leah right behind her. And Jimmy fixin' to shoot somethin' just because he ain't found nothin' yet to shoot. He think he has to shoot, so he pointed the gun at me."

"Whyn't you take it out of his hand, then?" It was Grand, standing in the doorway from the dining room. There was Aunt Mattie Belle leaning around her to see. Grand was speaking to Uncle Donald, a hand on each hip.

"With what?" Uncle Donald said.

With that, some of the men hurried out the front door and some went around Grand in the doorway, going the other direction. One or two tried to get out the front-room window on the side. It didn't have a screen. But Grand quickly rolled a Sunday newspaper and smacked them good around their ears.

"What you think this house is—a sideshow?" she demanded. "No Mars invasion. Yall *invaded* my clean house, shoot!"

Willie Bea hurried to the kitchen just to see if there were treats other than Grand's cake. Toughy Clay followed. No treats. Grand must have forgot.

Good, she thought again.

Willie Bea and Toughy slipped out the back door. Right at the rear of the house was the well. It was true—when they went around, the top piece of a well stone was clear to the side of the well. At the edge of the yawning black hole stood Aunt Lu and Aunt Leah. They had their arms around each other. They were peering, sort of, leaning slightly, looking over at the well hole. Aunt Lu was moaning and whimpering. Neither of the women was saying anything about jumping. Aunt Leah was quiet now, in her lovely gown and heels.

Behind them, facing the gathering men, was Uncle Jimmy. He had his shotgun in both hands, held across his body.

"What in the Sam Hell do you think you doin'?" asked Gramp Wing, coming up to Uncle Jimmy.

"I'm a-guardin'," Uncle Jimmy said, "that's all."

"A-guardin' what?" said Gramp. "And why the Sam Hell you take that cover off the well for?"

"Well, Leah and Lu want to look. I want to see what's maybe there, too," Uncle Jimmy said. You couldn't tell his expression, not enough light from the kitchen, but he sounded sheepish to Willie Bea.

Then Grand was there with her rolled newspaper. "Listen here!" she said. She climbed up on Uncle Jimmy's feet to get taller. "I'm not havin' this foolishness." She smacked Uncle Jimmy across his nose with the newspaper. It had to upset him, if it didn't hurt him, too, Willie Bea thought.

"Give me that gun!" Grand went on. She grabbed the gun out of Uncle Jimmy's hand, cracked it open like she'd been doing that all her life, and took out the shells and let them fall on the ground.

Quickly, Uncle Jimmy bent to retrieve them. Grand wasn't standing on his feet then. She had backed up so she could have room to scold. "The idea!" she said. "I know where the star-gazin' comes from, too." She glanced at her daughter Leah. It was hard to tell if Aunt Leah was looking at her mother. "Don't know why you always got to *perform* so," Grand Wing continued. Back to Uncle Jimmy. "Don't you say a word," she told him. "Cover up that well right now. And not a word! Donald, you get over here and help. Riley Knight, Jason Jr., you get over here, too. Go take Leah and Lu inside. Get them somethin', some cordials, down their throats, if they not got any better sense."

Grand glanced up at the sky. She leaned back and gave a long look. So did Willie Bea. It *was* smoky up there. Different and dark and smoky.

Grand shook her head and went inside.

"They never got to jump," Toughy said, a shade disappointed, as Riley and Jason Jr. soothed the two aunts. Aunt Lu and Aunt Leah were silent, leaving the wellside. Willie Bea looked longingly a moment after Aunt Leah.

"Have you seen Big and Little?" She turned back to Toughy, whispering.

"Sure," he whispered back. "They gone over Big's with Hewitt," he said peevishly. Willie Bea knew they had not allowed him to go with them.

"Think I'll go on over to Big's," Willie Bea said, loud enough for Jason Jr. to hear, going up the kitchen steps with Aunt Leah. Hearing her, Jason Jr. looked around, but he had no time for her now. He went on inside.

There, she thought. If anybody wonders where we went to, he'll remember I said over to Big's. Well, Mama is too strict. Said me and the chaps not to leave over home.

But Big and Little and Hewitt could leave. Nobody always watching *them*.

"Did you happen to tell Big and Hewitt and Little about the Martian you saw?" Willie Bea asked Toughy. They watched as Uncle Jimmy and some men eased the well cover back on.

Toughy looked sharply at Willie Bea. "What be wrong with that?"

"Come on!" she whispered. While most were inside and those outside were busy with the well cover, she and Toughy slipped away.

"Where we goin'?" Toughy wanted to know. They crossed the Dayton road and walked in shadows, dark shades of night among the trees around Willie Bea's house. They skirted the light coming from the upstairs windows. There was just a low lamp light on downstairs, Willie Bea noted. They heard the front door open as they moved silently around the back.

Papa! Willie Bea thought. And clutched Toughy's arm to stop him. They crouched by the back porch, where Willie Bea had hidden in the morning. So long ago! she remembered. They heard her papa cross the Dayton road.

"Now," she whispered. They raced for the barn.

Just inside the door there was a light bulb. Willie Bea pulled its chain, and a dim light came on. "Just a minute," she whispered, "we'll be out of here."

They could hear the hogs beyond the closed door. Willie Bea bent over and got the stilts. "Help me," she called. Toughy Clay came slowly over. "You can use Bay Sister's," she told him. "They're just as tall as mine.

Thank goodness my little sister didn't see me leave—that poor child."

"What you doin', Willie Bea?" Toughy said.

"Don't you see?" she said. "We can *stride* right on over to the Kelly farm on these!"

"Oh, no," he whispered, and hung his head.

She looked at him. "You know the way. You have been there?" she asked him.

He nodded, but he did not look up.

"Then let's go!" she said. "I've got to get there first!" She found a flashlight on her papa's work table. "You carry it," she told Toughy.

"How'm I gone carry a flushlight and work them stilts, too?" he said. "And in these two sheets I got on?"

"It's a *flash*light," she said, "and you carry it in your pocket."

"You carry it in *your* pocket," he told her.

"I don't *have* any pockets. Now, come on!"

"Wait, I got to do somethin' with these sheets," he said.

"I can take one," she told him.

Toughy unwound the sheets. He had a wool shirt and the same corduroy knickers on beneath. He had on men's long stockings below the knickers. Toughy gave one sheet to Willie Bea. He tied his like a cape around his neck, letting it hang down in folds from his shoulders. Willie Bea did the same.

"Superman!" he said, without much conviction. The cape would keep him warm. Toughy wouldn't think of refusing Willie Bea. After all, she was inviting him with her, and most of the time he seemed to get on her nerves.

Couldn't find her all day, too. He'd have to ask her some-time where she'd hid. And it was his own fault he had talked about the Kelly farm. He had no one to blame but himself for that kind of lie. It had just slipped out—a Martian man!

Resignedly, he followed her over to the porch, where they could get on their stilts. They used the thick rubber circles out of Mason canning jars to hold their feet in place on the wedge footrests. Toughy helped Willie Bea first. Then, when she was on her stilts, she steadied his stilts while he fixed his feet on his wedges.

"You go first," Willie Bea told him when they were ready. "You got the light, and you know the way."

"All right, Willie Bea," he said softly. There was no point in arguing. He did know the way over there, no lie. And moving, scared, was probably a whole lot better than standing still, scared to death.

"Hope we don't run into nothin'," he said under his breath.

"Hope the Venus man is still there," Willie Bea whispered to herself. "Oh, just don't let him leave all of a sudden. Don't let Little see him. Oh, let a Gobble-un get her."

Watch out, Little, here comes the Venus Star!

**10** They strode the dark world, stilting. Willie Bea and Toughy Clay were out in the countryside. They were along roads, and through the fields whenever it was possible for them to get over fences.

The velveteen night and the distant, cold stars were what they could see traveling with them. They imagined they were alone on earth. Willie Bea could feel the loneliness in her heart and soul, and more than once she wished she was home.

Why'd I start this dumb, fool journey? she wondered.

They both imagined beings from another planet just out of sight in the dark.

Toughy Clay didn't dare turn around to check their backs, for fear he would see something beyond belief and fall. "You ever think what's gone happen if one of us fall off these dang stilts?" he whispered loudly to Willie Bea.

But she was thinking hard, and when she answered, it was not about one of them falling. "The evening star of Venus could be falling down on us this very minute," she told him.

"You think so?" he said anxiously.

"Sure," she said, "and maybe that Mars is falling down, too. They say it is red and *mean*, boy!"

Wonder what is really going on, she thought. And if the United States army can't stop them space men, what will happen to *us?* And why come everything is so awful quiet all around?

She felt strange, as if they were being watched. She was about to warn Toughy and tell him to shut off the flashlight. The light bobbed along with them. It was a weak light, batteries wearing out. It barely lit the side of the road. But it was what they had and a comfort in the dark.

Suddenly, there was a burst of flames close to a fence in a field they were passing. The flames grew rapidly into a huge bonfire. The fire flowed up and licked a pile of brush and brambles, crackling and sizzling hotly.

A gun went off with a roar. It was such a shock, all that fire and then the shot.

"Am I hit?" Toughy cried. He lost his grip on the flashlight, but he kept his balance. "Oh, lordy, somebody shootin' at us!"

"Shhhh!" Willie Bea said. "Be quiet!"

The flashlight clattered and rolled on the road. It broke open and its light went out. They would have to leave it.

There was no way to get down and then back on the stilts again.

"Halt! Who goes there!" a rasping voice yelled.

A man came toward them from the bonfire. He leaned on the fence and aimed his shotgun right at them.

"Oh-muh-god!" Toughy whimpered.

Willie Bea's heart thudded and skipped. She lost her breath; got it back, ragged and gasping.

"It's us. We're only kids!" she managed to call out.

"Well, balls-a-fire! I almost 'bout to give you some buckshot," said the man. "What chu kids doin' out chare!"

A woman who looked to be his wife came up beside him. "An' so tall—stilts!" she said.

"Don' chu know they is Martians spreadin' they sin all over this land?" said the farmer. "Get on in your home!"

He was a skinny farmer. There were some young kids about half Willie Bea's age around the fire now. She didn't recognize them or the farmer from this far side of town.

"We're on our way now," she hollered across. "But have you seen anything?"

"How can I see anythin' when you make me light up muh far-er fer nothin'?" hollered the farmer. "Git on away from here 'fore I git my dandurf up! Now git!"

Willie Bea and Toughy went, striding as fast as their legs and arms propelling the stilts would take them, their capes bouncing.

"No!" hollered the farmer after them. His children and wife commenced shouting. "That's the wrong way! You're headin' the direction of that Kelly farm. That's where the Martians is. . . ."

But Willie Bea and Toughy were gone. They were in the dark, invisible in the night.

Her hands and face were cold now.

So cold! she thought. Glad for the capes of sheets!

Out here where there were only cornfields, the cold seemed to sift down from the sky into the ground and come up again. Willie Bea longed to stop and just take stock of things. Her muscles were mighty sore, holding on so tightly to the stilts. Her fingers cramped her, and her legs were stiff and chilled. They were starting to ache.

"Maybe we oughtn't to come out here," she said softly. All was so still around them. "Toughy, maybe we ought to just go on back."

Toughy strode ahead of her. They had slowed somewhat, for thick trees along the road blocked out the bonfire light behind them. They crossed onto a narrower gravel strip with fields on either side. Gravel was tricky beneath their stilts. Willie Bea saw that there was no fence on either side of the gravel road.

"This is a private road," Toughy told her.

"Whose private?" she asked him.

"It's the Kelly private," Toughy said. "Cuts right through the corn, and they own it. Can say who walk and stride on it, too." Toughy had never been on the Kelly road before. But he recognized it from the years of stories he had heard about the farm.

"Are we that close? Keep your voice *down*," she whispered.

"Look there," Toughy said. He stood, shifting back and forth to keep his balance.

Willie Bea shifted, too. But she was better at balancing

than Toughy was. Just arm pressure and flexing leg muscles was all that was necessary. And once in a while moving the stilts an inch or two. "Look at what?" she said.

"There. Come over here," Toughy said.

She came up beside him. And what she saw made her feel like someone had shut down all her tiredness. Had turned off the cold of her hands and face. She didn't realize she was shivering, but the cold had got way under the hobo costume she had made.

They were on the private Kelly road and it had risen over a hillock. At first Willie Bea looked down at the reach of land.

"Is it the ice-skating lake?" she asked in the softest voice. Who could tell anything in this deep night?

"Uh-uh," Toughy said. "I hear the lake is on the other side of the house. Here is only the fields on each side of the private road."

"Well, I'm glad of that," Willie Bea said.

She thought to look up, gazing across and beyond the black land-reach to where there had to be some sort of hill. Over there, situated high and handsome, was the biggest house Willie Bea had ever seen. It was enormous. And it was lit up like a carnival, like a birthday cake.

"Havin' a Halloween ball?" she asked in awe.

She thought she heard strains of music coming from the mansion.

"Think they just own a lot of light," Toughy said. "Think they must be listenin' to their Victrola phonograph."

They don't even know the Venus ones are here! Willie Bea thought.

"Did you hear that?" she said. "Did you hear them laughing over there, them Kellys?" she asked Toughy. Her voice was dreamy and faraway.

"No," he said. "They don't act like they care about Martians, though."

"Not Martians," Willie Bea said. "They are from Venus."

"That's what you said before. But how you know that?" he asked her.

"Aunt Leah read my palm and she found in it the Star of Venus. Aunt Leah says it is a sign of great good luck."

"You sure?" Toughy asked. But he knew anything Leah Wing told was true. Everyone knew that Leah Wing was the best fortune lady ever did live among the people. And rich, like the Kellys.

"So you lookin' for the Venus ones. So, see what they have to say to you?" Toughy asked.

Willie Bea nodded in the dark. "I don't know what-all will happen," she said in a misty voice. She never took her eyes from that Kelly mansion of enchantment. "But maybe it will stop the attack from them. Maybe if they see there's somebody here that has the Star of Venus . . ." Her voice seemed to drift off on the air.

"I don't know," Toughy murmured. He imagined it could be true. In the deep dark of Halloween night, the Kelly farm was a magic kingdom. Invading men from Venus were *boldacious* monsters, close about. Watch out! Anything could be true.

"Where'd you see the monster?" Willie Bea asked. "Was it over there? You can see some big, dark trees by the light from those windows."

Toughy shifted uneasily on his stilts. He cleared his throat, about to tell his lie again, when Willie Bea said, "Come on! We'll follow the road closer."

It was deep, dark going, and their stilts made grating sounds on the gravel. When they were down there, it didn't feel or look much different than on the rise. It was cold. The cornfields looked full of tall rows of dark.

"There's no lake that I can tell," Willie Bea said.

"I told you. Say the lake is on the other side of the house," Toughy said.

"Well, you don't have to yell," Willie Bea told him.

"I'm not yelling!" he yelled back.

They were both yelling. Noise, a deep rumbling, was coming out of the ground. Willie Bea couldn't hear herself breathe, or think.

"What's that?" she hollered at Toughy.

"Don't know. Can't tell where it is or what it is!" he hollered.

It was getting closer. Willie Bea thought she saw something. Like the blackest night moving.

"You see that?" she thought she yelled. Her mouth moved, but she couldn't hear what came out. "Toughy!" she screamed.

"Willie Bea!" he was screaming back. "Willie Bea!"

Now they could guess what the noise was. The great black dark that moved was one of the monsters. It was a rolling, ear-splitting, outlandish alien. And huge.

The thing must have turned a corner in front of them from behind the house, somehow. It had turned toward them and they saw its evil eye.

159

An awful, white, wicked, round eye. It could have been its heat ray, but it didn't hurt them. It was just blinding.

"Wait! I got the Star!" cried Willie Bea.

The great black dark came straight for them. And another huge blackness came on behind it. Giants as tall as houses, tall as trees, on the move.

Another one came after the second. Two of them marching, rolling behind the first. They spread out to the left of the first one. Their blinding eyes outlined the first one. Illuminated it for Willie Bea to see plainly that it was a deadly, monstrous alien.

"It's true! It's an invasion!" Toughy was yelling. "Run. Run, Willie Bea!"

Willie Bea couldn't hear him. She couldn't move. She was transfixed by the monsters. The first one's neck wasn't in the center of its body, where it should have been. It was on the right *side* of it! The long neck was like a wide stovepipe jutting out of its side. Its head that fitted on its neck was *all* V-shaped.

Suddenly, it seemed that the first monster spoke to her. She was staring into its awful eye, into its noise. The darkness moving one by one was overpowering.

All went quiet inside Willie Bea. She no longer heard the monster's roaring noise. Its sound of voice was right with her, like it was all around in her head. It seemed to be right by her, right in her ear.

"Huh?" Willie Bea said, staring wildly into the evil eye.

"Willie Bea, I come here, too. I got here late. I was looking for you. Heard you shouting." Spoken loud and as clear as a bell in her ear.

The white eyes of the monsters coming on held her

hypnotized. She thought she told them, "Look. I hold the Star of Venus in my palm. Turn off your rays. Don't fight. We only want to be friends!" She held up her palm for them to see.

"Willie Bea, we'd better get back. You coming back with me?"

The first monster was now to the left side of the road. Its head on the side, on its long neck, was coming right at her.

"Oh, no, I can't go back to Venus with *you!*" she told it.

"You're just scared and tired. Follow me close behind."

The second monster was passing along beside the gravel road. Willie Bea looked up at its head.

"No! Get away!" she hollered.

Then she was backing away from the third monster. She thought its light was bearing down. "You leave me be!" She flailed her arms backward and one stilt leg slipped in the gravel. She twisted, trying to untangle herself from the foot wedges. She was falling. Something grabbed at her. She saw the last monster's head turn in her direction. Its light was full on her. It was coming for her.

Willie Bea, falling. And something, someone had hold of her, was falling with her. She hit the ground, falling hard on part of someone. Something struck her a glancing blow on the forehead.

All went dark for Willie Bea. The dark filled with glowing comets and stars. Great planets of Venus and Mars. All such colors of worlds, pumpkin yellow and orange in a Halloween universe.

Willie Bea opened her eyes on an alien standing over

her. She thought she saw its V-shaped mouth: "Willie Bea! Are you hurt?"

"No. I won't go back with you, either," she told it. "I like my own world."

"You hit your head. It knocked you silly," the alien said.

Willie Bea's head started hurting. Suddenly, she felt cold all over. Her legs were aching. Her hand with its Star felt numb as she came to.

She saw a great light. It was upon her and the someone who stood over her.

"Where . . . ?" was all she could think to say.

She heard fast footfalls on the gravel. She lifted her head and was blinded by the white monster-light. The monster made its roaring sound, but it wasn't moving now.

"What happened?" it hollered, sounding frightened. "What are you kids doing where we are harvesting? Did we hit someone? . . . Oh, little child!"

Willie Bea saw a man in the light. He knelt beside her. "Did the combines scare you, child? We might've run you over!"

Willie Bea was damp and clammy from the gathering cold and mist. Tired and confused, she closed her eyes. Her insides flopped and the inky night of a dizzying universe returned.

Where a giant black cat sat on a pumpkin world. Where aliens were Kelly kings. They took away the Star in her palm. Willie Bea was so small, so unimportant. They made her polish their V-shaped crowns of gold.

**11** It was Monday, the day after trick-and-treating. Willie Bea was still lying down. There was school, of course, but she didn't go. She had a knot in the center of her forehead as big as a walnut. And it felt bigger than that. They said that one of her stilts must have hit her as she fell to the ground. Or rather, as she hit Big. For it had been Big Wing she had partially fallen on, so they had told her. He had taken hold of her and had fallen with her.

The town doctor, Dr. Taylor, had come to fix her up, at the start of a long, wakeful night—last night. Willie Bea remembered most of it in a kind of dreamy reverie. As soon as they got Willie Bea home last night, her mama had sent someone over to Dr. Taylor's with the message that

Willie Bea had a huge lump on her forehead; all she wanted to do was sleep. That Willie Bea might have a concussion.

Dr. Taylor had sent a message back that he would come as soon as he could, said Willie Bea's mama to her papa. But he had a lot of work this night, what with folks seeing monsters everywhere, and accidentally shooting at their toes, and driving their Model A's into old sugar maples that they mistook for Martians. The messenger said—it had been Uncle Jimmy, he had the car—that the doctor would do the diagnosing himself, when he came. The messenger standing at the door and not coming in that late nighttime. Willie Bea was glad of that.

After Uncle Jimmy left and before the doctor had come, Willie Bea's mama said to her papa about how she felt foolish at believing there was a Martian invasion. Not all believed it, her mama told her papa. Not Grand Wing. Not Donald Wing. Certainly not Riley Knight, she didn't think. At that point, she had smiled at Willie Bea's papa. Saying, some must feel even more foolish, thinking it was Nazis invading. And her papa answering, some most certainly did feel foolish. He had looked slightly embarrassed.

Dr. Taylor always came eventually, after Marva Mills called him. He was an old, old man. But he got around. He knew people like Willie Bea's mama and papa didn't send for a doctor unless there was a serious question and they didn't know what to do.

Dr. Taylor came at about one o'clock in the morning. Willie Bea was on the couch in the living room with a blanket spread over her and a soft bedpillow under her neck. Her mama had fixed a chunk of ice in a dish towel and was holding that on the bump. The ice felt cold. It kept Willie Bea awake when all she wanted to do was sleep, she hurt so. She guessed her baby brother and Bay Sister were fast asleep upstairs. She remembered wishing she had stayed safe and sound asleep like them.

Willie Bea kept pushing her mama's hand away. But Marva wouldn't stop applying the ice. Soon, Willie Bea gave up trying to stop her, and she stayed awake the whole time.

Dr. Taylor came in and he was old. To Willie Bea, he looked just like Moses on her Sunday School cards, but without a long beard. Wonderful white hair and sparkling eyes. Tall. Tall enough for heaven. Folks said he was eighty-seven, but to Willie Bea he looked closer to one hundred. His baby-fine snow-white hair reached to his shoulders. His black greatcoat came almost down to his ankles. He had on a green woolen scarf and he wore a black Homburg down low over his forehead. He wore old-fashioned leather spats that covered his feet from instep to ankle. He came in and bowed in greeting and for Marva to take his Homburg hat. He had his black bag in one hand and his cane in the other, so he couldn't very well take off the hat himself.

His daughter, who drove him everywhere, came in and took his coat and scarf over her arm, taking his cane for a minute while she did so. Then she gave Dr. Taylor back his cane. Willie Bea watched as he shifted his black bag from one hand to the other while his daughter got his coat off. Just seeing him made her feel better.

Dr. Taylor wasn't paying any attention to his daughter,

who was Vermilla Taylor and a nurse. She never had married and was called an old maid. Said to be a very good nurse, too. He wasn't paying any attention to Marva or to Willie Bea's papa, who was over there on the piano bench. Willie Bea recalled that someone else had sat on the piano bench. It was on the tip of her tongue who.

When was that? she wondered. But she hadn't said it out loud.

Then Dr. Taylor was beside her. He had pulled up a chair next to the couch. She could smell the wonderful, minty scent of him woven through the aroma of medicines on his clothing. She listened to the way he breathed hard through his mouth. She looked into his rosy face and his bright blue eyes behind his glasses.

"Well, Miss Willie," he said gruffly, "let's see if there's fever. The way you are shivering . . ." He took out his thermometer and put it in her mouth. While he took her temperature, he felt her pulse, listened to her heart and examined the bump on her head.

He grunted. "What you want to hit yourself in the head for?" he said, frowning. She knew he didn't expect her to answer with a thermometer in her mouth. Dr. Taylor was joking with her, Willie Bea knew. He always joked with his patients.

"It was the stilt that hit her, Doc," said her father on the piano bench.

Dr. Taylor grinned, winking at Willie Bea. "He don't think I know that!" he whispered loudly. Her papa had to hear. "He thinks I'm too old to find out things for myself!"

Willie Bea remembered all this now through the pain of

her forehead. That stinging, cold pain made everything come clear.

Her father had looked sheepish. "Now, Doc . . . ," he said. But Dr. Taylor waved him quiet with one hand, never taking his eyes off of Willie Bea.

He placed his hand on what felt to Willie Bea like a bump the size of an orange on her forehead. And getting bigger. "Does that hurt?" he asked her.

His hand was as light as a feather, even when his gentle fingers probed.

She shook her head. But it did hurt her, oh, it did!

"Cat got your tongue?" he asked her.

And again she shook her head.

"Well. Don't feel like talkin', do you?" he said in sympathy. "Don't blame you at all! No, sir. Do you know what kind of *Willie* it is can walk on stilts over a mile in the dead of night?" he asked her.

Had it been that far? Then Willie Bea listened as closely as she could, what with her head aching and her back hurting so. She felt that any minute Dr. Taylor would prove that she was someone special.

"It has to be a pretty brave Willie to do all that!" he said, still in a loud whisper for her mama and papa to overhear. "Wonder why Willie had to do all that!" he said. "'Cause of them monsters over at the Kelly farm?"

Willie Bea nodded. And then her mama and papa and Dr. Taylor and Vermilla Taylor had a brief discussion about how the monsters had only been on the radio and that the invasion was some actors. Willie Bea hadn't caught much of the discussion, she was so tired. She'd understood even less of it.

Then Dr. Taylor had taken the thermometer out of her mouth.

"Well, I'll be!" he said. He looked hard at Willie Bea until his eyes swam with amusement. "Not a bit of fever! Sakes, this child ain't sick with a grippe. But that bump is nasty and I don't see why she's shiverin' so. Maybe some exposure. It was cold last night! Now, Willie, I want you to tell me. How many fingers do you see? Four?" Dr. Taylor held up three fingers.

Willie Bea shook her head. She held up three of her own fingers to show she knew the right number.

"Anything else hurting you?" he asked. "Talk, child!" he commanded, and Willie Bea talked right away.

Her voice had come, soft and as weary as she had felt. "My back hurts so. It hurts just awful."

Dr. Taylor looked hard at Willie Bea's mama, standing, clutching her hands.

"I never thought," Marva said nervously. "I saw that bump . . ."

"That's why you're the mama and *I'm* the doctor!" he said triumphantly, his eyes twinkling away.

"Now, Father," scolded Vermilla Taylor, hovering. She lived in fear that folks would take her father's bluntness the wrong way.

The doc hurumphed at Vermilla and turned back to Willie Bea.

"Let's see that back," he said. Willie Bea had to turn over and loosen her pajama bottoms. Somebody had already removed the sheet she had worn like a cape. She looked around for it, but she didn't see it.

She unbuttoned her shirt, then lay quietly on her stomach. Dr. Taylor lifted the shirt away from her back. She heard her mama draw in her breath quickly. Willie Bea began to cry, fearing she had a broken spine.

"Now see what you done?" Dr. Taylor said to her mama. Marva quieted at once. "Child will mess up her hobo face, too!"

"Just some bruises," Dr. Taylor said soothingly to Willie Bea. "A few scratches that we'll put a salve on." With some cotton he put something that stung a little on Willie Bea's back. Then his blue-veined hands moved expertly over the scrapes, working a salve in. His hands were not quite warm on her back.

"That hurt?" he asked. "You tell me if it hurts."

"And probably the strain on the muscles of all that stilting and falling on your cousin," Dr. Taylor added. "Big Wing! Now, *he's* something! What a *monster* he turned out to be!" He had laughed his head off at his own joking.

They say laughing makes you live longer, Willie Bea had thought, and thought again now, as she woke up for the tenth or eleventh time this day.

Dr. Taylor knew all the Wing families, as he knew all the large families in the town. He had delivered all of the Wing children, he had lived that long, Willie Bea knew. It didn't matter how rich or poor folks were, how black or white they were, she realized, he served them all. He was the only doctor any of them would have. He knew it. He was proud of it. And he did his best, which was good enough. Quite fine, really, Willie Bea's papa would say.

Wonder if Dr. Taylor serves that Kelly farm, Willie Bea thought. They are a large family, so I hear.

Now she was awake again. She knew what day it was. Monday. End of October. She was upstairs in her room, although she didn't remember how she'd got there.

Must've been sometime after Dr. Taylor and his daughter left, she thought. What time was that? I remember he kept me talking and talking a long time. He played a game with me. He had Mama sing me some songs. He said after a long while that I was all right, not much of a concussion that being a child wouldn't cure, and he gave me something, to soothe my throat, he said. But I didn't have a sore throat. So why did I take it—and swallow it?

After that, it was morning; it was light out, anyway. The house, the street outside, so quiet. Mama came with a tray. But I didn't want anything but toast and my camomile tea. Mama calls it cambric tea. But it hurt me all over just to reach for that toast and tea. Ate the toast, but I left the tea after a sip or two. So hot and good! Mama took away the tray. Left the plate and cup.

Bet my papa carried me up here, thought Willie Bea. Her papa would often carry her up, or Bay or Bay Sister, when one of them fell asleep in the chair. Her long legs dangling as he carried her. Sometimes she awakened, was comforted that it was her papa holding her, and went right back to sleep on the stairs, her head on her papa's shoulder.

Willie Bea was in her bedroom now, in the big bed, in the middle of it. Bay Sis probably had gone to school,

Willie Bea guessed. And Bay Brother would be downstairs, underfoot of mama. Willie Bea recalled vaguely hearing him come upstairs to see her, making it almost to the door before her mama caught him and shushed him. She had taken him by the hand back downstairs.

Carefully, Willie Bea stood the hurting long enough to turn on her side. So now there would be no one to annoy her in her illness for the whole day.

She had to smile at the thought of her illness. I have a bad bump, feels as big as a . . . as a . . . hedge ball of a osage tree! she would say to Little when she saw her.

Little!

Willie Bea rubbed her forehead, avoiding the bump. She squeezed her eyes tight closed. She hadn't allowed herself to think about the night before because she was sort of upset about it, afraid to go over it in her mind.

Oh, that darkness night of monsters! Had it all happened? Had she and Toughy Clay really seen that bonfire and the farmer who told them to git? Did they go on to the Kelly farm?

'Course we did, she thought, scrunching in a ball under the covers. And you know what happened then!

She had been keeping herself from thinking about it.

Afraid I won't see it the way it was. Afraid those men from Venus never happened, the way Mama says. When did her mama say that?

Her mama and papa telling her things last night sometime. She remembered now, she had the feeling then that they all, even Dr. Taylor and Vermilla, thought she might feel ashamed of herself. Feel foolish, like her mama and papa did. But she didn't. And they were telling her it was all right, she needn't feel bad about feeling ridiculous or ashamed.

But she never did feel that way. Why should she?

All of them having another discussion, telling her:

That what she called the Venus men, and what they called men from Mars, and what Toughy Clay had called an invasion, *hadn't happened*. That the whole thing, the panic and all, *had been nothing more than a radio play!*

On a radio show.

Aunt Leah fainting, and Mr. Hollis (that was who, on the piano bench) lifting her in his arms. Gorgeous Aunt Leah of fortune and wealth! And Aunt Lu Wing ready to jump down the well.

How could that be nothing more than a radio play? she thought, pulling the covers up over her face.

She made night come under the covers with her, where the air was warm and space was endless in the darkness. Finally, she had the proof of the Kelly farm. What kind of radio play would have the Kelly farm on it!

What I saw wasn't a play or a show, Willie Bea thought, shivering under the covers. The noise I heard. The great white eyes I saw. And *them*, talking to me! Toughy was there, he said it was an invasion. He saw it all. Talked to me right in my ear!

Willie Bea closed her eyes again. A scene flooded the dark redness behind her eyes. She couldn't seem to dam it up and hold it back. There was the white eye of the monster. There was somebody standing over her. There was this man saying . . .

"No!" whispered Willie Bea. "I don't want to hear him. He was just trying to fool with me."

But the man's voice wouldn't go away. "*What happened? What are you kids doing where we are harvesting? Did we hit someone? . . . Oh, little child!*"

No! "*Dum-de-dum-de-dum!*" Willie Bea hummed, so the voice would go away. She sat up in bed. "Ouch! Oooh! Ahhhh!" She sucked in her breath from the pain in her back and legs, even in her arms. It was an aching hurt all over. A tired soreness of muscles and bruising scrapes. "Oh, man!" she said as the aching rid her of the voice.

The bump on her head was an impossible soreness, with shaking aches on either side of it. Oooh! Am I gonna die? No. Dr. Taylor said I'd be all right. And that old doctor never lied.

Willie Bea knew a story that proved Dr. Taylor never lied. Say he once told a daughter that her olden mama hadn't "kicked off" until the daughter had helped the dying mama lie down.

Can you imagine saying something like that to some weeping woman who has lost her only mama? Willie Bea thought. Better not say anything like that to *my* mama! But Grand Wing will never ever die.

Willie Bea was sure of that. Looking around her room, it was so nice to be safe at home. Warm and safe! With covers and a mama to bring you buttered toast.

What time is it? she wondered. She saw that the cup of tea and the empty plate for toast were still there on the chair. But the house was a long-past-breakfast house. She could hear the radio on downstairs and distant music as the shows changed. It had to be late in the morning or even noontime. Had the twelve o'clock whistle blown? She listened hard.

173

And heard it blowing! Just as she thought about it, it went off.

Well, I am special, aren't I? I can tell when a whistle will blow!

She found herself reaching for the cup of cold cambric tea before she had even thought about it.

I want it, she thought, cold or not. But when she had it—she found that when she moved slowly, it didn't hurt her so much—and tasted it, she didn't want it at all.

What do I want, then? she wondered. I'm not even hungry. Am I? I am so tired!

She was tired. Exhausted, and all she had been doing was sleeping.

She was about to burst into tears out of temper and hurting all over, when someone knocked softly. Willie Bea froze, watching the door. Her mind slowed to a ghost walk. And all she could think of was monsters with one eye. Was it possible for some monster to slip in your house and up the stairs?

Oh, me, no, don't let . . .

But it was no monster. What was left of the fears from the night before dissolved for Willie Bea at the sight of Bay Sister, home from school for lunch. Bay Sister had on her red jumper and one of Willie Bea's hand-me-down blouses underneath. She looked nice. All at once Willie Bea felt sad, strange inside, having stayed in.

Out in front of her, Bay Sister held a blue dinner plate with a sandwich on it. Willie Bea knew the sandwich was for her. And knew what kind of sandwich it was at the moment she spied Big, behind Bay Sister, carrying the tray. The tray had a steaming bowl of soup on it and a cup of something else hot. Big came in like he was walking on eggs.

"Move that stuff! Hurry!" he told Bay Sister, his eyes cutting to the chair next to Willie Bea's bed.

Quickly and with one hand, Bay Sister put the teacup and saucer and the bread plate on the floor. Gingerly, Big set down the tray. "Whew! I did it!" he said, straightening up again. He seemed to tower in the bedroom, he was so big and the cciling was that low.

"Hey, Willie Bea," he said. He looked kindly at his cousin, and his best friend, his look seemed to say. "Oooh, man! That some knot you got on you head."

"It hurts like the dickens, too," Willie Bea said. "Hey back. Hey, Bay Sister."

"Hi you?" asked Bay Sister.

"I'm feelin' better, some," Willie Bea said. "I been sleepin' a lot. Dr. Taylor gave me somethin'."

"Yeah?" said Big. "They say you can't remember, and not to make you think about the scary stuff last night." Immediately, he put his hand over his mouth. Bay Sister kicked his ankle, Willie Bea saw her.

"We brought you some food," Bay Sister said. "See?"

"I see," Willie Bea said.

"A egg-salad sandwich. You love egg salad," said Bay Sister. "And some veg'ble soup and some chocolate Mama made. Bay is havin' some chocolate downstairs. Only he have some on his shirt and on the tablecloth more than in his mouth. What in the world all happened last night, Willie Bea?"

Before Willie Bea could answer her, Big said, "I carried

that tray up them stairs and didn't spill *nothin'*." He looked pleasantly surprised.

"I see you did," Willie Bea told him. "And thank you very much, Big."

She sat up straight. Big had to lift the tray again. Very carefully, he placed it on Willie Bea's lap. Bay Sister took the egg-salad sandwich off the plate and put it on the tray. "There," she said.

"Have you all had some lunch?" Willie Bea asked.

"I'm not hongry," said Big. Willie Bea eyed him. Then she handed him half the sandwich.

"Take it. I can't eat so much. I already had toast," she said.

Reluctantly, Big took the sandwich and tried not to eat it in one gulp. Willie Bea gave the other half to Bay Sister. She gave them each a sip of her chocolate. So much passing back and forth nearly exhausted her. She sighed heavily. "Don't know *what's* a wrong with me today."

"But what happen last night?" Bay Sister asked. "Papa ran in, say all you kids was gone to the Kelly farm. And then we have to go home from Grand's, no trick or treat or nothing. Papa unlock this house for us. And then him and Uncle Jimmy . . ." But at a slight signal from Big, Bay Sister shut up.

"I'll go down in a minute," Bay Sister said quickly, "eat and get back to school. Willie Bea, we made Halloween masks today. I have to color mine, yet. I'll bring you another sandwich before I leave."

Willie Bea looked at Big as she sipped the soup.

"I ain't gone back this afternoon," he said. "I don't feel like gone to school any more today."

"Uncle Jimmy better not find out," Bay Sister said.

"I ain't worried," Big said.

Little marched in just as Big spoke. "Ain't worried 'bout what?" she said. She had half a smoked-ham-and-mayonaise sandwich in one hand and an apple in the other. She was looking at Willie Bea. She was panting as though she'd been running, and she had. All the way from Uncle Jimmy's house, where she'd grabbed some lunch, and then eating it on the way to Willie Bea's house. She saw the knot on Willie Bea's forehead. She looked away and pretended she had not seen it.

She's even jealous of my bump! Willie Bea thought.

"That Kelly foreman bring you home," Little said.

Willie Bea stared at Little in a calm way, although she didn't know what Little was talking about. What was a for-man?

"Yeah, and we in the car with him, and we spy your papa on his way to Kellys'," Big said, helping out Willie Bea, "'cause Toughy already run all the way to get some help. What he think somebody gone do against some monsters? He come upon my daddy and Uncle Jason in the car. They see him and they stop the car. They on the way to Kellys', too. Daddy has his shotgun and Uncle Jason has his pickaxe."

Willie Bea stared at Big. She was still confused.

"And I see my daddy's auto when we in the foreman's sedan," Big continued. "The Kelly foreman take care of that big ole farm for Mr. Kelly. He run the place himself, boss of the other mens."

"Yeah, huh!" Little said. "That foreman ridin' this gret big machine. And two other men ridin' each a gret giant machine. Call it a one-man, all-machine *combine!* It cut the corn up by *automatic*, it just new to buy it right now." She eyed Willie Bea. "And *you* think them real giant machines some monsters—hee!"

"Shut up, Little!" Big said.

"Well, she did!" Little said.

Bay Sister stared from Big to Little and back, but she was afraid to look at Willie Bea.

Willie Bea gazed around the room. Right away, she took up the soup bowl and commenced sipping soup from the rim. All of her attention seemed focused on eating the soup, which gave her time to think.

What was Little talking about? Willie Bea recalled hearing *combine* someplace before. She had a sinking feeling. And put together the voice of a man in her head—*"Oh, little child!"*—with this for-man Little and Big spoke about.

"You don't know anything!" finally Willie Bea thought to say.

"I know you a sight," Little said. "Daddy say oughtn't to let you out at nighttime. You moon-eyed. You the one cause me and Big to be over there in the first place. I was smart. I left my stilts and walk, me and Hewitt."

"Little, it's not true she cause us to be over there," Big said.

"Big, the reason you went way over there is 'cause you sure Willie Bea be comin' one time!" Little said. "And she get there before we do 'cause you got lost!"

"Little, whyn't you be quiet?" Willie Bea said softly. "You givin' me a headache."

"Daddy say you a scaredy-cat. I knew them things was

big machines—what else could they be? Shoot," Little said.

Willie Bea suddenly felt terrible.

Machines. She forced the thought of them to the back of her mind.

Uncle Jimmy. Having an uncle, especially one like Uncle Jimmy, calling her a scaredy-cat and moon-eyed was almost more than she could take. She felt just awful about it. To have a relative say something like that!

And have another one repeat it, she thought, that was even worse. She might not have a lot of things, like Little had, but she certainly had her pride.

And now Willie Bea held her head high. The knot on her forehead was hurting and it would be sore for a good while. But she looked Little straight in the eye. Wouldn't let the corners of her mouth turn sad. Not one bit. She stared Little down, until Little had to turn away.

"Ho-hum," Little thought to say. She looked up at the ceiling. "I got to go to schoo', and after schoo' I got to get ready for that Halloween parade. Ummmm. Mama gone iron my Little Red Riding Hood so it just look fine and I win first prize."

"Mamuuuh!" Bay Sister yelled out the bedroom door for her own mama. She was outraged that Little would brag about her costume again. "Little is actin' up in front of Willie Bea in our bedroom!"

That took Little by surprise and she slid out the door and down the hall. In no time, she was on the stair landing and out the front door.

Willie Bea knew that Bay Sister hadn't yelled quite loud enough to be heard downstairs. But Little didn't know that.

**12** "Answer me, Big," Willie Bea said. Her voice was barely above a whisper, but she could hear herself clearly in the quiet bedroom. So could Big. He sat there at the foot of her bed. He was facing the mirror, but he did not look at it. He looked down at his hands. Willie Bea could see only one side of his face.

"Big?" she said. She held tightly to the covers up to her neck. "What did I see out there? Did you see what I saw? Did you? Have you talked to Toughy Clay? You talk to Toughy and you'll know that Little has to be wrong. Not machines! No, sir!" At last she allowed herself to think about machines. "Can machines talk to me?" she asked.

Big sighed deeply. He wrung his hands. "Well, which?" he said.

"Which what?" Willie Bea asked.

"Which question you want me to answer?" Big said. "You ask all so many questions. I can't answer every one.

"Haven't talked to Toughy," Big went on. "Haven't seen nobody today, 'cept Mama and Daddy and Little. S'pose Hewitt and Uncle Donald and Aunt Mattie Belle left already, way early this morning."

Willie Bea thought about her cousin Hewitt a moment. "Was he with you last night? Did you see us—me and Toughy—out there? Did you hear the man from Venus talkin' to me? I didn't see you or Little or—" Willie Bea stopped. The image of someone standing over her in the dark swam in her thoughts. She squeezed her eyes shut, then fluttered them open.

"There you go again," Big mumbled. "Askin' so many questions, I don't know which."

"You're not foolin' me!" Willie Bea hissed. "And you're suppose to be my friend!"

"Now, Willie Bea—"

She didn't let him finish. "You can just get out of here, too. I don't want you here, Big!" She covered her face up to her forehead with the covers.

"Willie Bea, come on, where'm I gonna go?"

"Well, you don't need to hide out here," she told him. "You won't answer me, you can leave right now!"

"Okay, okay," Big said. He still wouldn't look at Willie Bea. He seemed to be talking to the air in front of him. "Only, I thought they was from Mars."

"What? You saw them, too?" Willie Bea whispered. She sat up and clutched the sheet around her shoulders.

"Well, you just said they were some Venus men," he said. "Only, I heard tell they was s'pose to be from Mars."

"Then you did see them!"

"Oh, man! Oh, me!" Big said. "How I know what I seen out there? Willie Bea, goodness, it was so dark and scary. At first it was just like you say . . ."

"Giants, and moving, rolling toward us! Their one-eyes shinin'," she said, "their roaring noise."

"Them things sure were loud," he said, nodding. "Shoot, and comin' at us, too. I was right behind you, Willie Bea. I was on my stilts. I picked you out right there in front of me when those lights of theirs was shinin' comin' at us."

"The Venus men," she whispered. "The giants of Venus."

"Willie Bea . . ." Big smoothed his hand nervously along the coverlet on her bed. "Can't we just drop it now?" His voice was low. "Whatever you want. Just, don't let's talk about it no more."

"Big. We saw them, we're the lucky ones!" Willie Bea said.

"Whatever," he said, unwilling to argue. "Willie Bea, just if you could help me get my bow and arras back?"

"Well, sure!" she said. "Does Papa have them? Did your papa give them over? I never believed he would give them over. When did he give them over?"

"There you go again, Willie Bea! How'm I s'pose to know when and so forth?" Big said. "I'm just sayin' I think your daddy got them. Will you look around, ask?"

"Sure!" she said. "If they're here, I'll get them back for you. But, Big, you mustn't use Bay Brother any more."

"I'll never do that again," he said. "I swear I won't."

"All right," she said. "We are friends!"

"Yeah!" Big said. He turned to look at Willie Bea. He

melted with happiness on seeing her smile. "Willie Bea," he said softly. He could find no more words. But all that he felt for his cousin was in the sound of her name.

Willie Bea lay there and Big sat there, as happy as he could be. He listened to Willie Bea talk and he enjoyed everything she said. She showed him that Star of Venus in her palm. Even though Venus was a planet, it was called the evening star.

Big had to squint close to see it. He shook his head. "You awful brave, girl," he said, "and not be afraid to have somethin' like that in your hand."

They talked about getting him a bull's-eye to aim at, instead of aiming at her little brother. "Maybe we can make one," Willie Bea said. "Does Little have some crayons? I mean, some real good ones?"

"She got a black crayon and maybe a fat red one," Big said.

"Maybe you could get hold of them. We get a good-size piece of oilcloth and cut it out, round," she said.

Big stared at her for a long moment. "Maybe you could be my bull's-eye," he said. He looked at her fondly.

"Really? Me?" she said. "But won't I be too tall?"

"No," he said, "just different."

"Really? I never thought to be . . . No, Mama wouldn't like that either, Big. It's the idea of you usin' a person to take aim on. She's afraid you might hit somebody."

Big was shocked at that. "I would never hit *nobody!*" he said. He looked hurt. "You know I never miss."

"I know that and you know that," she said. "But grown folks only see what *could* happen."

Willie Bea heard her mama's step at the top of the stairs. She was on her way to the bedroom. Marva came in and went quickly to Willie Bea. She placed her hand lightly on Willie Bea's forehead.

"Hey, Mama Marva," Willie Bea said, joking.

Her mama smiled at her. "I see you are feeling better. How's that bump feel?"

"Hadn't even thought of it for a while until you mentioned it."

"Huh! That's good," her mama said. "Your daddy will be home soon, about an hour, along with Bay Sister," she thought to add.

"That late!" Willie Bea said. Where did the time go?

Marva Mills studied her nephew's profile. "Big, are you hungry?" she asked.

He looked sideways along the bed, smoothing his hands on either side of him on the coverlet. "Maybe I am," he said. His Aunt Marva didn't seem to be still mad at him.

"You decided not to go to school today," Marva said, a statement of fact.

"Thought I'd keep Willie Bea some company," he said.

"That was kind of you, Big," Marva said.

Shyly, he smiled down at his hands. He did so love his Aunt Marva. She was so the best kind of woman, next to his own mama, he was positive.

"But if Jimmy asks me, I will have to tell him you were here," Marva said.

"Mama, why come?" Willie Bea said.

Marva gave her one look and Willie Bea knew why, had known all along. Her mama had to tell the truth to Uncle Jimmy or anyone who might ask for the truth. That was the way things were. Big knew that, too.

"It's okay," Big said. "Just if he ask you."

Marva smiled fondly at her nephew, more like an overgrown, shy son. So shy! "Let's hope Jimmy doesn't ask!" she said, laughing. She wasn't angry at him any more. Too much had happened.

They all laughed, conspirators.

Big went downstairs with his Aunt Marva to get something more to eat. He came back after a while with a cup of hot chocolate. He asked Willie Bea why she didn't drink hers, but she just shook her head, she didn't want any.

She fell in and out of sleep, hearing Big's delicate slurpings of the chocolate. It was nice to have him there at the foot of her bed. Like he was guarding her. She supposed he was, in his way of sitting with her. It made her feel safe. Somewhere inside, the monsters were with her. They were going, farther and farther back they went, but they would not leave her.

Willie Bea was sound asleep. Big got up as silently as he could and quietly left her. He went downstairs into the kitchen, where he said goodbye to Aunt Marva.

"I'm goin' now," he said, as softly as he could. For Aunt Marva had her back to him. She was at the refrigerator and he didn't want to scare her with a loud voice all of a sudden.

"All right, Big," she said, turning to him. "Thanks for sitting with Willie Bea. You cheered her up."

"Yes, ma'am," he said. "That's all I wanted to do, too."

Going out, he saw Bay Brother sound asleep on the couch. He hadn't noticed on his way into the kitchen. Big went on home, his hands deep in his pockets. Little would be home soon and she would surely tell his daddy on him. Still, he trudged steadily on. Tattle-telling was just something he had to put up with. But seeing for himself that Willie Bea was going to get well made it all right.

Willie Bea's papa came home a little late. When he got up to Willie Bea's room, he was loaded down with Bay in his arms, newspapers in one hand and a large brown sack of something in the other.

She woke up right away when he came in. "Papa," she said sleepily, "hey."

"Hi you, Wil' Bea?" piped up Bay Brother.

"Hey, Bay," she said, and smiled at him and her papa.

"Hey, Willie Bea?" said her good papa. "How you feelin' now?"

"Oh, okay," she said. "Big was here." She didn't say a word about Little. "Bay Sister went back to school—she wasn't tired out like me." She didn't tell that Big hadn't gone back to school.

Her papa let Bay down on the bed. At once Bay crawled up next to Willie Bea and stared at her face. "Oooh!" he said. He saw the painful-looking bump on her forehead, which he had been hoping to see all day.

"It's plain sore now," Willie Bea told him, about the bump. "It felt big as an orange this morning. Now it feels about the size of a walnut." She laughed up at her papa.

"It's not quite that big now," said her papa. "Have you looked at it in the mirror lately?" He had let the newspapers slide onto the bed. He set the sack down and then shoved everything over so he could sit down.

Willie Bea shook her head. "I don't want to see," she said. Then she jumped up and gazed in the mirror. It was comical to see her move so fast. She got out of bed and went up close. Her papa laughed at that. She looked at herself and she didn't hurt all over any more, either."

"Goodness, it's not as bad as it feels," she said, about her bump.

"Most hurts aren't," her papa said. "Commere," he added. She came back to the bed and he folded her close. She snuggled on his shoulder, wrapped her arms around him. "You had yourself a time last night, didn't you?" he said gently.

"Oh, Papa, don't scold me, please!" she pleaded. Great tears filled her eyes and slid down her cheeks.

"Now, don't you cry," her papa said. "I'm not gonna scold—that would be like closin' the barn door after the herd has snuck away. I guess you are just my adventure-some one. You have to go out and see."

"Well, I do," she said, leaning back to look at her papa. She wiped her eyes.

"I was just worried you might get yourself hurt out there."

"But, Papa, you should've seen the Kelly farm! Oh, my goodness, what a swell place it was!"

Her papa nodded. "And still is swell! Which reminds me," he said. He reached for the sack.

"Candy!" Willie Bea said.

"Yay! Candy!" hollered Bay Brother.

"The foreman of the Kelly farm, a Mr. Branner, brought it over just now, too," her papa said.

The sack was full of everything she could think of. Chocolates, candy corn, homemade peanut-butter fudge, each piece wrapped in wax paper. All kinds of bright hard-tack candy. Apples and oranges. Walnuts and other nuts in their shells. There were enough Halloween goodies for her and Bay and Bay Sister to keep them happy for a week.

"Goodness!" said Willie Bea. "He did this for us?"

Her papa nodded. "He did it for you because you were hurt. You know what is a foreman?" he asked.

"The one who runs that Kelly farm," she said.

"Yes, and he was worried about you," her papa said.

"He was?" said Willie Bea, eyes wide, all thought of tears vanished.

"What was all right about him," said her papa, "he wasn't peeved that you all were out there on private property. He knew I knew you all shouldn't have been there. He was just upset at the thought of what might have happened. You see, he and his men were harvesting the corn. They, or the Kellys either, didn't know anything strange was going on.

"Well, it was sure nice he came by with these treats," said Willie Bea. She and Bay each had a piece of chocolate.

"Now that's all before supper," her papa said.

"Can I come down for supper?" she asked him.

"Yes, but stay in bed until then, okay?"

"Okay," she said, and climbed back into bed.

Jason Mills took up the sack, but he left the newspapers. "Come on, son," he said to Bay. "You and I have some chores to do."

"That's right!" Bay said. "Chores, my piggies!"

"Yep, your piggies have to get fed, Bay," Willie Bea told him.

"Yep!" he piped, looking mighty eager.

She and her papa grinned at Bay Brother, who was

more fun to be around than a whole circus. He just enjoyed everything so much, even the dirty work of slopping pigs and hogs.

"Quite a one, your brother," her papa said to her. Bay grinned.

"Yep," said Willie Bea.

"Like his sister," her papa said.

"Yep!" Bay piped, and they laughed at him.

Her papa paused at the door. He took something from the inside pocket of his jacket. He had Bay hand it to Willie Bea.

"The foreman showed me that, said I could borrow it to show you," her papa said, as Willie Bea looked at the pamphlet. "Says about those new combine machines they have over there at the Kelly place. Cost a fortune, each one of them. And they are the newest farm machines anywhere, and they are right there over at the Kellys'."

He paused again. "Willie Bea. I brought you all of the papers telling about last night. You weren't the only one seeing . . . monsters. Seems like the whole county was in an uproar. Even that foreman, he said somebody shot at the combines. But he never knew why. Nobody over there had the radio on. One of his men was grazed by a bullet. Broke the glass of that little compartment the driver sits in to steer the machine. One of the headlights was knocked out of each machine. They didn't realize until later. Can you believe that? It was like the whole country went crazy last night.

"But it was just a radio play," her papa went on. "Even *I* got caught up in it." He grinned sheepishly. "Thought it was the Nazis invading. Boy! What the imagination can do to you, I'll tell ya! Just a radio show. The fellow—

Orson Welles, his name is—put on a radio show on this Mercury Theatre on the Air, you know. He's the one that was the voice of The Shadow for a while."

Ohhh! The Shadow! Willie Bea thought, and wondered about this Orson with such a scary voice.

"A radio play of this writer's, H. G. Wells' *War of the Worlds*. And folks thought it was real. You look, Willie Bea, it's all there in the newspapers," her papa said, "all that Aunt Leah told us. She heard the radio play, that was all."

"Willie Bea," he said, "I'm not telling you what to believe. I am showing you the facts. And facts are the truth."

With that, her papa gave her a look of love, of sympathy, and went out, closing the door behind him.

Willie Bea sat still. She stared at the closed door with a clothes hook just low enough for her to reach when she stood on tiptoes. She heard her papa grunt, lifting Bay in his arms to carry him down. All of a sudden, she heard the outdoors, sounds she had not been aware of the whole day. And yet they were sounds she was used to. The hogs squealing occasionally. A car going by. Kids, noisy, running home from school. Then she listened to someone coming up the stairs. By the noise, she knew it was Bay Sister. The door swung open.

"Hey! I'm home again!" Bay Sister said.

Willie Bea looked down at her lap. She let the pamphlet lie there on her knees, lightly touching its edges with her fingers.

"What's a wrong?" Bay Sister said softly.

"I'll be down in a while for supper," Willie Bea said.

Her throat felt scratchy and full. She didn't want to talk any more.

"My room, too," Bay Sister said, pouting.

Willie Bea gave her a hard look. "You get on down the stairs!" she said, harsher than she had meant to.

Bay Sister backed out of the door and ran for her mama downstairs. Willie Bea knew that her mama would tell Bay Sister to leave her alone awhile.

I'll make it up to her later on, Willie Bea told herself. But now she had to think. Her papa. All the papers. This pamphlet. She had to look at it. Had to see it. You couldn't avoid facts, her papa always did say.

*Combine* was what it was about, that pamphlet. And other farming machinery. Right on the front was a drawing of the latest combine design, with a man at its steering wheel, and all of its parts named.

*"How a Combine Works,"* was printed in black above the picture. A combine was house-tall. It had a fan, it had a straw rack, a chaffer, a sieve. It had a grain bin. It had a grain auger and elevator, sort of like a wide chimney. It had a feeder beater and a cutter bar. It had attachments for harvesting corn.

What a combine did was cut a standing crop of grain. Then it separated the grain. (Willie Bea read this inside the pamphlet.) It threshed the grain, and discarded the straw and the husks. The combine that was pictured on the front of the pamphlet was self-propelled. It could cut a crop twenty feet wide at one time. And it could harvest an acre in from five to eight minutes.

Goodness! Willie Bea thought. Even she, who had

known nothing about a thing called a combine yesterday, knew today that it was a wondrous machine.

A whole acre!

But it was something else about it that really caught her eye.

The combine had a second auger on one side of it, like a very large stovepipe about twenty feet long. It was an *unloading auger* used when the machine was ready to unload the corn into waiting wagons or trucks. Willie Bea stared at it.

The unloading auger went up so high and out away from the combine on a slant. Such a long, long neck it had. At the end of the neck was this peculiar shape, like a triangle.

The strangeness of it, so high above her. So awfully scary. At the height of it was fitted that triangle.

Willie Bea dropped the pamphlet. She felt an awful fear rising. She was filled with terrible sensations, visions of the dangerous night before.

There at the Kelly place. The thing coming at her. A hulking, huge blackness moving. Rumbling. Bending, turning, reaching for her in the one-eyed light of dark.

Monster of the night!

The horrid, V-shaped head.

**13** It might have been night in Willie Bea's bedroom. With the window blinds drawn on the clear October light, it seemed perpetual evening along the dim wallpaper design—vases of fading flowers in neat rows. There was a light on, not so bright. Willie Bea could see well enough. She leaned close to the newspaper she held. The pamphlet she'd been reading had slid to the side.

It had taken her some time to get over that panic feeling of the night before. And now she'd had her fill of combines.

Make me sick to see that picture, she thought, shoving the pamphlet aside.

There had been the monster as big as life. Just a silly

farm machine. It was almost impossible to believe. But facts were facts.

Willie Bea's mouth tasted sour. She got up, went out, found some water left in the water pitcher on her mama's dresser. She drank right out of the pitcher. Next she used the chamber pot. Her legs felt none too sturdy.

That's because I've been restin' so long, she thought. Goodness, the way I feel, I wish the world *would* end.

She felt pretty awful. Not so much from bumps and bruises, but from having to face herself. Finished, she hurried back to bed.

"I think I made a fool of myself," she told herself. "I think Uncle Jimmy is right about me." Sadness came over her and she felt as lonely as she could be.

Back in bed, she forced herself to look at a newspaper. The Xenia, Ohio, paper, October 31, 1938.

"That's today," she said out loud. But her own voice was no comfort now.

"'MARS INVADES U.S.,'" she read the lead headline in a whisper, "'BUT BY BROADCAST.'"

Willie Bea sighed, steeled herself inside and read on, her lips moving, whispering. It was a forlorn sound in the otherwise silent room.

*"Washington, October thirty-first."* That's today, Monday, Willie Bea thought.

*"Chairman Frank R. McNinch of the Federal Communications Commission today wired the Columbia Broadcasting System for a copy of the radio script and a transcription of the broadcast 'The War of the Worlds' broadcast over the Columbia network last night with startling results.*

*"The chairman said the program, which aroused the entire country with its portrayal of the imaginary attack on Princeton,*

*N.J., by mysterious monsters of Mars, will be considered at an early meeting of the commission."*

Willie Bea studied the words and understood them. Not monsters of Mars, she thought vaguely. That Orson fellow is sure gonna get it, too.

The paper went on to say that the radio program caused thousands of people in every part of the country to believe that the eastern United States had been invaded by creatures from the planet Mars. It was the first engagement in a "war of the worlds." But the hysteria was not limited to the East.

*"In Indianapolis, an unidentified woman ran down the main aisle of St. Paul's Episcopal Church, crying, 'The world is coming to an end.' The congregation was hastily dismissed.*

*"In Toledo, Ohio, three persons fainted at telephones while trying to call police.*

*"But in the East . . ."* Willie Bea skipped part of the account. *". . . Several persons came forward to swear they saw the rocket land and 'strange creatures' climb out of it."*

Well, I'm not the only one, she thought. She didn't feel so bad then. Other folks saw things, too.

*"In Newark, N.J., hundreds fled from two city blocks, carrying what possessions they could snatch up . . ."* Well, I'll be! she thought.

*"Telegraph companies reported that they were delivering telegrams from as distant as California inquiring of the fate of relatives . . ."* Goodness!

*"'They're bombing New Jersey,' one excited voice informed police.*

*"'How do you know?'*

*"'I heard it on the radio, then I went to the roof and saw the smoke from bombs drifting toward New York. What shall I do?'"*

Willie Bea read on, but there was no answer from the police as to what that person should have done.

I would a gone down in the basement away from the bombs, she thought. But maybe that person's basement was flooded. Willie Bea's own basement usually had at least an inch of water in it. It wasn't completely dug out. Half of it was four feet of good black soil gone sour from too much standing water. They used the basement only for storing her mama's canned goods on high wood shelves away from the ground water—grape jelly, tomato jam, string beans and young cucumbers miraculously changing into sweet pickles. Every winter they'd hear *pop, pop, pop* in the night as unsettled glass Mason jars under too much pressure exploded. Good thing her mama canned more than enough, too.

The last account of the Mars invasion Willie Bea read came clear from New York, the paper said.

"The New York Times *reported that it had received a telephone call from a man in Dayton, Ohio . . .*" Well, I'll be! Only eighteen miles from here, Dayton.

Willie Bea hadn't been to Dayton yet. She had no reason to go. But she was sure she would get to go sometime. Her papa had mentioned something about the circus coming next summer and seeing that great star gorilla, Gargantua, in his air-conditioned glass cage. Willie Bea just couldn't picture some animal living swell in some glass room full of cold air. It just didn't make sense to her.

". . . *who wanted to know what time the world was going to end.*" That was what the man from Dayton, Ohio, wanted to know.

Just like Aunt Leah, Willie Bea thought. Aunt Leah had kept saying the world was coming to an end.

Willie Bea laid the paper aside. Leaned back and closed her eyes. Darkness swam there, making her dizzy. Her eyelids fluttered open quickly after that.

Am I sick? Or just hungry? Willie Bea couldn't tell what was wrong with her.

Just don't feel right, is all. She felt awful, out of sorts, jumpy. A bit ashamed now, she wasn't sure why.

What have I done? Did I do something wrong? She closed her eyes again. Now she could keep them closed. Wish they'd call me to supper. But nobody called her. Not yet time, she supposed. No early feast with lots of relatives, like on Sunday-company.

She thought she knew when the sun went down, when it began to get dark, but she might have been dreaming. She thought she heard—no, felt—the presence of someone on the other side of her bedroom door. She dreamed the door opening, somebody doing something for a moment at the clothes hook on the back of the door. And then opening the door wide so that the back of it was against the wall. A paper-rustling sound there.

Somebody came near. She felt the presence sit down gently beside her. She knew she wasn't dreaming now, although she was half asleep. Who was it? Her mama? She didn't feel like opening her eyes. In case it was her papa.

"Have you read the papers yet, Willie Bea?" he would ask her. "Did you study that pamphlet, Willie Bea? Now you know it all, Willie Bea. Facts are facts."

He would give her a lecture about making up things. About running off on adventures—walking high beams and stilt-walking with monsters. Actually, his lectures, like a teacher teaching, were his way of scolding. It always made Willie Bea feel sick inside at the thought of a serious lecture from her papa.

She dreamed it happened and she felt just so black and blue inside. She dreamed she ran off after a severe scolding. She stilted far, far away out into the ether that filled all space beyond the moon. Gramp Wing had told her about the ether, and so she believed. She dreamed a monster came and carried her up a closed staircase to the stars.

"Willie Beatrime," she dreamed someone called. Mama? Papa?

"Willie Beatrime, wake up!"

Willie Bea came to, but she kept her eyes closed. Huh?

"Willie Beatrime, baby!" someone whispered. Smoothed back her hair.

Suddenly, Willie Bea was aware of a scent sweeter than powdered sachet. It was a scent finer than the smell of roses in summer. A perfume of evenings in ballrooms, of silken evening gowns. The rare, rich fragrance of carnations eased Willie Bea's waking.

No. It couldn't be. "Aunt Leah?" Willie Bea opened her eyes. "Oh, my goodness, it *is* you!"

"Honey, and who else? This being Halloween," Aunt Leah said. There was laughter in her eyes.

She was dressed all in blue. Willie Bea couldn't believe how beautiful her outfit was. Aunt Leah had on what appeared to be a new fall coat. It was called a bouclé material dyed blue, a cloth with a tufted or knotted texture. It was just beautiful. Under the open coat, Aunt Leah had on a blue shirtwaist dress with a high collar. Pleated all around. It was lovely. And a gold pendant. And gold bracelets.

"Aunt Leah, my goodness!" Willie Bea whispered.

Aunt Leah hugged her, kissed her cheek. She leaned back to study her niece's face, that nasty bump.

"Baby girl, you sure suffered, didn't you?"

"Yes," Willie Bea said, holding close.

"Well, don't you worry. I taken all the blame."

"What?" said Willie Bea.

"Gettin' everybody all so excited." She watched Willie Bea. "I told your papa it was all my fault, too. Just now I told him."

"It's all right," Willie Bea said. "I didn't mind. But did he scold you, Aunt Leah?"

"Huh," Aunt Leah laughed. "Your papa don't scare me, honey, like he does everybody. Well, you know, knowing so much and everything. I think after while he was believin' somethin' himself." She smiled, eyes still playful, like she was still up to something.

"They told me over home what all happen to you," she went on. "I never knew you were the best of stilting in this whole county, Willie Beatrime."

"Me?" said Willie Bea.

"That's what everybody sayin', baby. Didn't you know you were the best?"

Willie Bea thought about it. "Not until last night I didn't."

"And that's not all you the best at, is it?" Aunt Leah said. "You take after me, there."

"What do you mean?" Willie Bea said.

Aunt Leah smiled. Willie Bea thought she was just beautiful when she smiled. Her face was so smooth, her cheeks and lips just the right amount of pink-rose.

"Oh, out there, what you chanced to see at the Kelly farm," Aunt Leah said.

"Yeah," muttered Willie Bea, "I chanced to see, all right. I made it up, you mean. Aunt Leah, it's all in the papers. That was a radio play you heard."

"I seen the papers," Aunt Leah said. She looked unconcerned, her kind eyes studying her niece's face.

"Does Papa know you are up here?" Willie Bea thought to ask.

"He does," Aunt Leah said, nodding. "So does your mama by now. I slipped by the kids—they were in the kitchen with Marva, cooking supper. Jason was by the radio in the living room."

"Well, anyway," Willie Bea continued, "what I saw was a new, great old big farm machine—three of 'em—called a combine. Never saw anything like it before in my whole life."

"And you've had such a long life, too," Aunt Leah said. She wasn't laughing, but her eyes were bright, shining. A shadow of a smile touched her lips.

"Uh-huh," Willie Bea said. She played with the rings on Aunt Leah's right hand until Leah took Willie Bea's hand in hers. "I feel just awful about what I done," Willie Bea went on. "And Big stayed the day with me. And now Uncle Jimmy will punish him, once Little tells he wasn't in school. And my papa took Big's bow and arrows, Big thinks. Everything's just terrible! How will I ever face everybody, especially Papa? Little's so mean. *She* gets to go to the parade in Xenia and wear a costume bought at the store. A Little Red Riding Hood."

It was all too much for Willie Beatrime. She lifted Aunt

Leah's slender fingers to her eyes and cried bitter tears into the palm of Leah's hand.

"Oh, now, baby, Willie Beatrime, don't do that. Don't cry so. I can't stand to see my baby cry!" Aunt Leah said. She really sounded like she cared a lot about Willie Bea.

But Willie Bea couldn't help it. She couldn't stop crying. Only when her nose started running did she let go of Aunt Leah's hand.

"Here, baby," Aunt Leah said, taking out a handkerchief. "Don't you cry any more."

Willie Bea took the handkerchief, but shook her head. "It's . . . too . . . pretty to . . . use," she sighed, sniffling.

"Use it," commanded Aunt Leah. "I *give* it to you. Got lots of *hankies*. Use it and wash it and hang it to dry. It will be like new."

"Real . . . ly?" Willie Bea said, drying her tears.

"Now," Aunt Leah said, "I can't stay too long. I've been all over the countryside today, seein' folks I upset last night." She grinned, and for the first time seemed slightly ashamed of herself. But quickly that look disappeared.

"Now listen to me, Willie Beatrime." Aunt Leah took Willie Bea by the chin and looked in her face. "You listenin'?"

Willie Bea nodded. "Yes," she sighed, looking red-eyed and sad-faced.

"Nobody's goin' to any parade tonight," Aunt Leah said. "Jimmy found out from Little that Big didn't go to school. Guess she sorry now she told, for Jimmy punish Big, and make Little stay home from the parade for telling on him."

"No!" Willie Bea said.

"Oh, yes," said Aunt Leah. "She'll have that Little Red Riding Hood next year, but not this year."

Willie Bea couldn't help giggling into her hands. For once, Little had got what was coming to her.

"Let's not laugh at our cousin, Willie Beatrime," sniffed Aunt Leah, but she couldn't help a tiny smile of triumph herself. "But what I want to say about something else," she went on. "Are you still listenin', honey?"

Willie Bea nodded again. "Yes, but what else do you want to tell me?"

"Just this," Aunt Leah said, her voice quiet and light as air. "Don't dismiss too soon," she said. "Know what I mean by that?"

Willie Bea shook her head. "No, Aunt Leah." She held the hankie tightly.

"I mean, don't think just because it was *just* a radio play, there was nothin to it. Don't think that because what you saw turned out to be *just* a combine, wasn't something *behind* it."

"Wha . . . what, Aunt Leah?"

"Honey," said Aunt Leah, "ain't it strange that that radio play come on when it did, and I hear it, and hundreds, thousands hear it? Ain't it strange that you see that combine and hear it talkin'? It's all *too* strange! There has to be something behind it, oh, yes!"

"Aunt Leah!"

Aunt Leah's eyes were bright. She wasn't looking at Willie Bea now. Yet she still had her hands on her. One hand on Willie Bea's arm and the other lightly touching Willie Bea's fingers clutching the hankie. Willie Bea was sure she could feel the strength, the power of fortune, through Leah's hands.

"Honey, when someone don't feel up to scratchin' in the ground with their hand, they will invent a hoe to reach for them what needs scratchin'. When a farmer can't cut the corn fast enough by hand, he'll go make him a *combine* machine to do it faster. Yes," sighed Aunt Leah.

"Baby, do you get my drift?" she went on. "Think of it. Think of it as a foretelling. Behind that *machine* of the radio and that *machine* of the combine and all so many folks just seein' monsters, Martians, things that *moved*, maybe was *them*. *Them* out there tryin' to tell us somethin'."

"Them?" whispered Willie Bea. "Them that talked to me?"

"Whoever talked to you," Aunt Leah said, "it was what was behind the talking. Talking just a kind of machine for our use, too.

"For someday, sometime, we are going out there," Aunt Leah said, "out into the ether. Up there in the stars."

"Aunt Leah!"

"I mean it, girl," said Aunt Leah. "You just wait! Maybe not in my lifetime, but certainly in yours. Why was there ever a story, *War of the Worlds*? Because somebody realize that we are goin' out there. We will go out to the moon and beyond. We will go to Mars and all so many stars and places."

"Venus!" cried Willie Bea.

"Sure, Venus," said Aunt Leah. "Not just this little world of ours. We aren't all of it, no, sir. Not just Roosevelt and that Hitler, either. Not just you and Little, too, or me or your mama and papa or this town or the Kellys!"

She smiled brightly at Willie Bea now. "Oooh, pretty Willie Beatrime!"

"Ohhh, Aunt Leah!" whispered Willie Bea.

"And I've got a surprise for you," Aunt Leah said, eyeing Willie Bea mischievously.

Willie Bea sucked in her breath. "You do?" She couldn't imagine what it could be. Aunt Leah had already given her a fine handkerchief. Would she now whisk her away to some hidden place where they would be together forever?

"Only if you understand—what?" asked Aunt Leah.

Willie Bea stared at her. "I . . . don't know what," she said finally.

"A surprise for you, if you know that good can happen and bad can happen."

"Oh, I know that," Willie Bea said, eager to please.

"But not just good and bad," Aunt Leah went on. "But that *anything* can happen. Anything under the sun. One night you look up, there's a monster, it's a combine, it's a monster. One time a space ship lands right there on the Kelly farm. And who's to say it can't! Who's to say it didn't? And why that radio play just then on this night in this world?"

Aunt Leah took Willie Bea's face in her hands. Her eyes were deep and dark. She kissed Willie Bea's bump. And whispered in her ear: "Don't ever say never!"

Papa says that sometimes, Willie Bea thought.

Aunt Leah got up. She waved at Willie Bea, although she was right there in front of her.

"Aunt Leah, do you have to go?"

Aunt Leah nodded. "Close your eyes. Don't open them until you count slowly to sixty. Okay?"

"Aunt Leah! What are you up to!"

Willie Bea closed her eyes, grinning from ear to ear. She was facing the bedroom door. She listened, but she couldn't hear Aunt Leah leave. What she heard was her door closing.

"Bye, Aunt Leah," she said, loud enough for Leah to hear. And then she counted. "One, two, three, four . . ." Out loud. She listened for Aunt Leah's car, but she didn't hear it.

Maybe she will stay awhile, she thought. "Fifteen, sixteen, seventeen . . ." All the way to sixty. It felt like a long time.

"Whew!" she said, and opened her eyes.

What she saw made her drop the hankie and cover her mouth with her hands.

Hanging there on the back of the door. It was the most beautiful thing Willie Bea had ever seen in her life.

It was a costume. Of stars. Of sparkles like silver. It was pink and silver. It had a fine pink netting called tulle over the skirt and bodice. The netting was sprinkled with the silver sparkles. And there was a silver rim around the neck and sleeves, a wide silver band around the full silk skirt that stood out. Underneath the see-through tulle was silky pink. A real, silky pink dress of soft folds. It looked like new, and it was, of course.

"Oh, it's beautiful!" sighed Willie Bea. There was a pink mask looped over the hanger by its rubber band. There was a pink wand made out of hard cardboard down in the dress sack that had been ripped open so Willie Bea would see the dress. The wand was sprinkled with silver stars, she saw, peeking down at it.

"And what's this?" Tenderly, Willie Bea lifted down her dress. She had to stand on tiptoes to do it. Behind her dress were two more sacks covering something. Willie Bea could see them.

"A costume for Bay Sister . . . and one for Bay Brother!" She couldn't tell for sure, but she thought Bay's was a pirate and Bay Sister's a gypsy girl.

"Oh, Aunt Leah!" Willie Bea shook her head, she was so thankful.

But her dress was the best.

"Just the most beautiful fairy girl!" she sighed, holding it up against her.

Then she noticed a note pinned to the paper.

"What in the world . . . !" She put the dress on the bed and took out the pin.

"From Aunt Leah," Willie Bea said. *"Dear WB,"* she read, *"Wave your magic wand and anything can happen. For next year, Halloween."* It was signed, *"Aunt Leah."*

Willie Bea stared at the note. She felt down in the sack. Took out the magic wand. She looked at it long and hard. And waved it. And waved it more.

"Nothin' happened," she said. She shook the wand hard. But nothing occurred that she could see. "Maybe somewhere, something's happening," she told herself. "I know!" The note said, *"For next year, Halloween."* "Wait until next year, when I wave my wand." She laughed. Do you believe that? she thought. "Well, why not? Anything can happen!" She laughed her head off.

Willie Bea hung up her costume and opened the door wide. It was wonderful how the costumes were all hidden with the door open. "Aunt Leah, you are sure something wonderful," she told herself. "Give you a big hug when I see you. You wait, I'll be just like you when I grow up!" She put the hankie under her pillow.

She went down the hall. At the head of the stairs, Willie Bea smelled a tasty supper aroma. And something so sweet and pungent.

"Pumpkin pie!" All of a sudden, she was weak with hunger.

She went down the stairs, sliding her shoulder along the wall. Downstairs, everyone was in the kitchen, nearly finished eating.

"Aw, why didn't somebody call me?"

"Somebody did," said her mama, "but you were busy." She gave Willie Bea a secret smile.

"Oooh! Guess what? Aunt . . ." Willie Bea stopped herself. There was Bay and Bay Sister, staring at her. Her eyes grew round and wide. "Ohhh, Bay! Oooh, Bay Sister! Have I got surprises for *you!*"

"'Top it, Willie Bea," said Bay.

"Bay, you said my name right," Willie Bea said. He looked at her as if she were silly.

"It always sounded right to him," said her mama.

"What surprises?" asked Bay Sister.

"Wait till I eat," Willie Bea said.

"How could you have a surprise?" Bay Sister said. "You been in bed all day."

Willie Bea smiled sweetly. "Anything can happen when you sleep in bed all day," she said.

And before anyone could think, she said to her papa: "Big says you have his bow and arrows!"

Her papa lifted his eyes to the ceiling before he thought. Over to his right, toward the living-room ceiling. "If I have them, Willie Bea," he said, "it's for a good reason."

Her mama and papa's bedroom was up and to the right.

Not over the kitchen. It was the front bedroom, over the living room, right where her papa had looked.

"Ho-hum," Willie Bea said airily. She took her plate and filled it from the pots warmed on the stove. Good turkey and noodles with peas. Biscuits. Willie Bea sat down. She saw the pumpkin pie over on the counter. None of them had eaten pie.

"I feel so good," she told them, buttering a biscuit. "My bump's gone down. I don't feel sore at all. I only missed one day of school, too. So did Big. Isn't it just so awful funny how things happen?"

Interested, they all looked on, her mama and papa, Bay and Bay Sister. The kitchen was a swell evening place to be. Warm and safe, with dark pressing on the windows. All Gobble-uns were safely out of doors. This would be a last witch-and-Gobble-un night of frights and scares for another year. It would go on without her.

Who cares?

Big's bow and arrows would be in the front bedroom closet. Or maybe under the bed. They would be in that front bedroom somewhere.

She stifled a grin.

Birds of a feather flock together! She and her cousin Big Wing.

Willie Bea giggled silently to herself.

She ate her fill.

# About This Apple Signature Author

VIRGINIA HAMILTON is one of the most distinguished writers of our time. Winner of the National Book Award and the Hans Christian Andersen Medal, she is the author of *M. C. Higgins, the Great* which was awarded the Newbery Medal, as well as *Sweet Whispers, Brother Rush; The Planet of Junior Brown*; and *In the Beginning*, all Newbery Honor Books. Her books of folklore include *The People Could Fly*, winner of the Coretta Scott King Award; and *Many Thousand Gone*. Ms. Hamilton has also written the novel *Plain City*, an ALA Notable Book and a *School Library Journal* Best Book; *Jaguarundi*, a picture book; *Her Stories: African American Folktales, Fairy Tales, and True Tales*, winner of the Coretta Scott King Award and an ALA Notable Book, a BBYA, a *Booklist* Editors' Choice, a *School Library Journal* Best Book of the Year, and an NCTE Notable Children's Book in the Language Arts. Most recently she is the author of the picture book *When Birds Could Talk & Bats Could Sing*, a *School Library Journal* Best Book of the Year, an *American Bookseller* Pick of the Lists, an ALA Notable Book, and a *BCCB* Blue Ribbon Book. She has been awarded the 1995 Laura Ingalls Wilder Medal as well as four honorary doctorates. She is the only writer of children's books to have been awarded a MacArthur Fellowship.

Ms. Hamilton is married to Arnold Adoff, who is a distinguished poet and anthologist.